Mari felt trapped

"I don't want to feel anything special for you, O'Neil!" she wailed. "I don't *need* complications like that!"

"Complications again," he observed, smiling at her. "You worry too much about them, but there won't be any with me. If enjoying each other's company doesn't make me special, then making love won't either."

"But what if it does?" Mari whispered. "Or what— and maybe I'm flattering myself—what happens if *I* begin to matter to *you*?"

"You won't," O'Neil answered, his voice calm. "If I thought there were any chance of it, I'd walk away, never to see you again. It's as simple as that."

Is it? she wondered. Was anything ever going to be simple between them again?

Elizabeth Barnes lives with her husband and son near Boston, Massachusetts. She likes to see treasures from the past lovingly restored and was instrumental in helping restore the local nineteenth century church after it was badly damaged by fire. Vintage cars are a long-standing passion of the whole family.

Now and
Forever

Elizabeth Barnes

Harlequin Books

TORONTO • NEW YORK • LONDON
AMSTERDAM • PARIS • SYDNEY • HAMBURG
STOCKHOLM • ATHENS • TOKYO • MILAN

Original hardcover edition published in 1989
by Mills & Boon Limited

ISBN 0-373-03056-8

Harlequin Romance first edition June 1990

CHAPTER ONE

SHE LAY suspended in that curious world between sleep and awareness, listening to the sound, wondering if the moment had arrived. She had often imagined that it would be something like this: a dull rushing sound, a faint roar which would gradually —even peacefully—consume her. Now, with sleepy detachment, she waited for it to happen.

Instead, and without warning, the sound abruptly ended. In its place she heard the lilting call of a bird and the lightest hint of a breeze feathering among the leaves of the maple tree beyond her bedroom window. Confused, she opened her eyes and through the dormer window saw the gold and slanting sunlight of early morning.

So, she thought, pushing back the covers and getting out of bed, this hadn't been the moment; she would have to wait a little longer. She smiled, ruefully and with a hint of self-consciousness, then went to stand by the open window. Below, the lawn she had mowed the day before was dappled with the play of shadows, darker green on green. Beyond the low stone retaining wall, her meadow stretched away, an unblemished sweep of sunlit green. The bird called again, the trill suddenly stilled as an unexpected shadow—a smoothly edged and elongated oval—swept slowly across the meadow.

Too smooth to be a cloud, she thought, leaning out of the window, looking up to see a towering swirl of colour. Blue and green, gold and scarlet—a magical kaleidoscope of colours drifting slowly over the house, just above the tallest reaches of the maple tree. She knew what it was and was away from the window, racing barefoot down the steep flight of stairs even before she saw the wicker basket or the flash of flame.

By the time she reached the lawn, the balloon was over the meadow, bearing slightly away from her as it slipped gently towards the ground. It was incredible, a breathtaking sight, lovelier and more alive than any photograph had led her to expect. She wanted to be closer, so she lifted the skirt of her nightgown and made the running jump over the retaining wall, landing in the taller grass of the meadow just as the wicker basket grazed the ground.

Suddenly the balloon's silent grace was gone, replaced by a leaden clumsiness. The basket bumped, then skidded slowly across the grass as the kaleidoscope of colour began to fall sideways, lose its form and buoyancy as it met the ground.

'Why didn't you keep going?' she called to the man who swung one long leg over the side of the basket and climbed out. 'I wish you hadn't stopped!'

'Why?' he asked, glancing only briefly in her direction. 'Didn't you want me landing in your field?'

'It wasn't that! It was——' But he had turned away, ignoring her to subdue the balloon, gathering in the billowing cloud of coloured cloth.

Silenced, she stood motionless, admiring the angular lines of his body as he bent to his task. He was a long man, all arms and legs, lean beneath the faded jeans and dark blue windbreaker he wore, his profile an impressive one, with thrusting jaw and imposing nose. Beaked or hawkish, she thought, searching for adjectives; imperious or even arrogant, the effect softened—if only slightly—by the way dark hair slanted, ruffled by the wind, against a high forehead.

'So.' He had finished with his work and now he straightened and turned towards her, his eyes hidden behind dark aviator glasses, a brief off-centre grin humanising a formidable face. 'Why did you want me to keep going?'

'Because it was magic in the air.' She gestured expansively, trying to show him what she had felt. 'Then, once it touched the ground, the magic disappeared.'

'Sorry, but I didn't have enough fuel left to keep the magic going. Your field seemed a prudent choice. Here,' he continued, reaching into the backet, producing a bottle and handing it to her with a courtly air. 'It's the custom,' he explained as she stared incredulously at the label—champagne, and Dom Perignon at that. 'Hot-air ballooning started in France, along with the idea of keeping a bottle of champagne in the basket—to placate the natives when you come down on their land. Or when you get them out of bed,' he finished pointedly, with another disarming grin. 'Surely that deserves some reward.'

'But I didn't mind!' She supposed—now that he'd reminded her of it—that she must look absurd in her nightdress, standing barefoot in the field, but that didn't seem to matter at the moment. It wasn't every morning that something so incredibly lovely descended into her life, and—given what she had thought was about to happen!—she had every reason to be happy. 'I'd have gotten up in the middle of the night to see this!'

'No need to. Dawn and dusk are the two best times. That's when the air is most likely to be calm,' he explained, 'and I expect you'll be seeing plenty more of me and my balloon. I've bought the place just beyond that ridge behind your house. We're neighbours now. I'm Angus O'Neil,' he finished, extending his hand.

'Our mysterious millionaire!' She laughed, shifting the bottle of champagne to free her right hand, watching as it was engulfed by his large, long-fingered one. 'We've all been dying to meet you—everyone in town has. You're not at all what we expected,' she confided as he withdrew his hand to take off his sunglasses, exposing her to the force of the bluest eyes she had ever seen. Lord, he was attractive, she realised instantly—large and vital and definitely an outdoor man. His hand had been hard, rough to her touch, and there was a weathered network of fine lines at the corners of his eyes. 'We had in mind a spidery, oldish man, someone with no sense and nothing to do all day but spend his money. You're not a bit spidery——'

'But I suppose I do look oldish, to a child like you.'

'Hardly! I'm nearly thirty,' she admitted, 'and you can't be *that* much older. Eight years, perhaps?'

'Close enough, and I spend most of my time working to make what money I manage to spend.' He paused to pull off his windbreaker, further disordering his hair. 'I keep reasonably busy.'

An understatement if she'd ever heard one, she decided, registering the broad shoulders and impressively defined musculature beneath the tan knit shirt. 'How are you going to get this thing home?' she enquired, changing the subject as she pointed to the remains of the balloon. 'Will you get more fuel and take off from here?'

'Nope. I've got a chase vehicle wandering around somewhere. They'll catch up with me sooner or later—if they can figure out this maze of roads. It must have thrown them when the wind shifted and headed me back home again. I'll wait for my crew, or walk back to my place if they don't show up.'

'Would you like coffee, or even breakfast, while you wait?' she offered tentatively, and was rewarded with another off-centre smile.

'I'd like both,' he accepted promptly, falling in step beside her as she started back across the meadow towards her little house, 'and it would be nice to know your name.'

'Mari Scott,' she told him, pausing to gather up the skirt of her nightgown while he took the retaining wall in one long stride. 'That's Mari with an i.'

'Different.' He took first the champagne bottle and then the hand he had freed, helping her up. 'Is it short for something else?'

'Short for Marigold. My mother had already used Lily and Violet and Rose. She was running out of suitable flowers.'

'Are you serious?'

'Deadly,' she assured him, walking on when he finally released her hand. 'It's the cross I have to bear.'

'A worse one for your brothers, I should think—if she tried to name them after flowers too. Or don't you have any brothers?'

'Just one—John, Junior. We call him Jack.' They had reached the stepping stone at the door, and now she paused to make a face. 'That's as in Jack-in-the-pulpit, a plant that passes as a flower. She's got us all in a garden. We don't match too well, and we bloom at different times, but we're all there.' She led the way into the house, then turned back to him. 'If you don't mind, I'll go up and throw on some clothes. I won't be long,' she promised, running lightly up the stairs.

Mari's house was a converted small barn; her

bedroom, under the sloping roof, had been the loft, and it was open, except for a low railing, to the living-room below. She had always liked the arrangement, but now she discovered that there was one disadvantage. For the first time in the nearly five years she'd lived here, she was wanting to dress while a man waited in the living-room below. She was willing to bet that Angus O'Neil was too much of a gentleman to look up and watch her; still, it seemed safer to gather up her clothes and retreat to the small bathroom built into the far wall. There she discarded her nightgown and put on a floral print cotton shift, one with a bodice she had smocked during the previous winter's long, dark evenings.

Then, about to emerge, she paused to study her face in the mirror. There had been a time, she remembered, when the prospect of the company of a man as attractive as Angus O'Neil would have necessitated much time in preparation—foundation, blusher, eyeliner, mascara, lip-gloss, just the right perfume to fit the occasion. And her hair! she mused with a reminiscent smile. Lord, her hair alone had been good for an hour or more. Long and light brown, it had taken all her skills with hot rollers and teasing comb to tame the unruly curls into some kind of order. Now she spent so much time outdoors that the sun had bleached the colour to a dark blonde, and she had given up trying to fight the curls, letting her hair fall casually to her shoulders, framing her face.

A face rather too long and too thin, she told herself, looking a little more closely for the first time in years. Stark reality had a way of clearing away the non-essentials, and five years before Mari had quickly decided that her appearance was one of the most non-essential things in her life. Now, knowing that an

attractive man was waiting below—another first in
five years, she acknowledged with a brief smile—she
was curious to know what Angus O'Neil saw when he
looked at her.

Her eyes were very light, a pale hazel which often
seemed grey or even silver. Her nose, like her face,
was a little too long and a little too thin, but her
mouth was wide enough to make up for
that—'generous', her mother had called it, with her
customary tact. 'And you've got nice cheekbones,
darling,' her mother had told her more than once.
'That's one thing to be said for having a thin face.
Even when you're an old lady, you'll still have that
lovely bone structure. Just think of that!'

That was one of life's little ironies, Mari told her
reflection, fighting the demons which suddenly
threatened. Damn! It had been months since she had
last felt their presence. She was a fool to let them in
now, a fool to be thinking about her mother's words,
and a bigger fool to have offered breakfast to Angus
O'Neil. The last thing she needed was a man in her
life. She didn't want to get involved with Angus
O'Neil; she couldn't let herself get involved with him.
Besides, for all she knew, he was a happily married
man, although she hadn't heard any talk about a
wife . . .

'Did you think I'd gone back to bed, or climbed out
of the window?' she asked brightly from the top of the
stairs. 'I didn't mean to be so long.'

'I don't call ten minutes long,' he told her, watching
with an appreciative glint as she came down the steps.
'Anyway, it gave me a chance to look around. I like
your place.' His gaze shifted to survey the room. 'It's
got character.'

It was kind of him to say so, and certainly Mari

liked it, but even she had to admit that the place lacked coherence. The couch was covered with a quilt she had pieced from a wild assortment of scraps, and further adorned by the cushions on which she had embroidered a few of her favourite designs. Close by were the two old wing chairs she had re-upholstered and covered with a multicoloured crewel tree-of-life design. There was further colour in her embroidered wall hangings which vied for attention with her collection of prints and framed photographs. As well as being colourful, the room was bright with light from the wide windows on three sides of the room.

'Perhaps it's a little too much,' she offered doubtfully when she realised he was looking at her again, 'but it pleases me—and I *always* do as I please.'

'A free spirit, in fact,' he observed with his off-centre grin, but his eyes were momentarily far away, and his tone was something close to wistful when he added, 'You're lucky.'

'But surely you're a free spirit too?' She managed a quick, curious glance before going into the kitchen to start breakfast. 'Any man who goes hot-air ballooning at dawn must be a free spirit.'

'But not every dawn,' he pointed out regretfully, following her, dwarfing the small kitchen with his presence. 'There are times when those dawns are few and far between.'

'When duty calls, I suppose, and you've got to make all the money it takes to support your expensive habits.'

'Lord!' He shifted uncomfortably. 'You not only *do* as you please—you *say* what you please.'

'Why not?' asked Mari, busy with the preparations for their meal, turning briefly to hand him plates and cutlery. 'Here, you can set the table.' Without him in the kitchen to distract her, she made quick work of the cooking. It was only a few minutes later when she announced, 'We can eat,' and edged past him to bring coffee and freshly squeezed orange juice to the round oak table by the east window. She went back for the scrambled eggs and Canadian bacon, edged past him again and had just placed them on the table when, behind her, she heard a muffled pop. 'Champagne—for breakfast?' she asked, eyeing him sceptically.

'Why not?' He reached for the glasses of juice, topping them off with champagne. 'This is a celebration.'

'Of what?'

'Of the fact that, for once in my life, the fun—or the magic, if you like—didn't end when the balloon landed. That's cause for celebration. Hot-air ballooning's a little like life, you see, and the trick is to make the feeling last as long as possible.'

'Or at least be as good as possible,' she contributed, suddenly grave.

'Yes,' he agreed shortly, as subdued as she, and there was the same far-away look in his eyes. Did he have demons too? she wondered, still watching as he forced a smile that gradually grew more real. 'But we haven't done too badly this morning, have we?' he asked, holding her chair for her with exaggerated courtesy before taking his own. 'I'll drink to that.'

'So will I.' She smiled, too, as they saluted each other with their glasses, her own black moment behind her.

'Tell me about yourself,' he commanded. 'Do you spend the whole summer here?'

'I spend the whole year here. I'm a native, or nearly so. I was born and raised about fifteen miles away, my parents still live there, and the rest of us are scattered around the immediate area. I'm the only one who ever left at all—when I was nineteen. I went off to New York to seek my fortune, but I decided to chuck the rat-race of the city about five years ago. I packed up and came back, but I didn't want to live at home, so I found this place and used up everything I'd saved to buy it.'

'And how do you support yourself out here in the middle of nowhere?' he asked, jutting chin resting on one hand, apparently totally absorbed by her story.

'Oh, I've got a thriving business—Marigold, Inc.,' she told him, laughing. 'I don't mind using my name for the business because the tourists think it's quaint. I started making craft items to sell in the shops in Stowe,' she explained, seeing his puzzled expression. 'At first, it was just wall hangings and cushions with embroidered or crewel designs. Then I added tote bags and belts and shawls and wrap-around skirts. Now I've got six women working for me, some making the clothes and some doing the stitches. I think up the designs, make the patterns, and do the first model. Then my sewing ladies take it from there.'

'In fact, you're an entrepreneur.'

'In a very small way, but I'm a lot more successful than I ever was when I was working for a big design house in New York.'

'And what's next?' he asked, chin still resting on his hand, that piercing blue gaze intent upon her face. 'Are you going to expand Marigold, Inc.?'

'No! There's no *next* for me!' But she had answered too sharply; she could see the question forming in his eyes and took refuge in being provocative. 'I'm not driven—the way *some* people are.'

'How do you know I'm driven?' he asked, taking

the bait.

'Your helicopter's flight path seems to go right over my house, so I hear you come and go.'

'And you don't approve.'

'I think you're a fool—I think anyone's a fool to make time that important, to be constantly having to rush about that way. Besides, I don't like your helicopter. It shatters my silence.'

'But I've got responsibilities—a business to run—and time is important to me,' he objected mildly. 'We don't all have the freedom to chuck the rat-race. I'm not in a position to do what you did.'

'I didn't think I was either, until I realised that I *had* to do it.'

'And what made you realise that?'

Careful, Mari, she cautioned herself; he's getting too close. 'I saw a sparrow by the IBM Building on Madison Avenue,' she began, choosing the half of the story she could explain. 'There's an atrium there— you probably know it—with flowers and trees in pots, and benches for people to sit on. It's like a small park, only all very sterile and clean, and behind plate glass. I saw that poor little sparrow try to fly in, to land on one of the trees.'

'And it collided with the glass,' Angus O'Neil supplied, a certain rueful comprehension lighting his eyes. 'But that happens often in the city, Mari. Surely you'd seen it before?'

'Yes, but it happened that day—and once too often for me.' She paused, remembering that fragile, lost and confused small bird, remembering just how fragile, lost and confused she had been feeling that day. 'I stood there and watched until the poor thing got up and flew away—probably trying to find Central Park—and I decided that I couldn't stay where things

like that happen. It wasn't worth it to be in a place so
. . . *uncaring.*'

'And so cruel,' he supplied absently, suddenly not
looking at her, but beyond—to where his own demons
waited, she guessed. 'Heaven knows, it can be
cruel . . .' He stopped, and when he spoke again he
was making an obvious effort, focusing on her once
again. 'Lord! I'd better be careful. If I spend too much
time with you, you might win a convert—which
would leave heaven knows how many projects
unfinished and people out of work. You're dangerous,
Marigold Scott! Did you know that?'

'I don't think——' she began, but he continued as
though she hadn't spoken.

'Still, I'm prepared to take the risk. I'm betting I'm
stronger than you are.' Unexpectedly, he got to his
feet, the tips of his fingers resting lightly on the edge
of the table. 'Since you like my balloon so much,
would you like to come up with me some time?'

'I couldn't,' she told him, relieved to have a valid
reason to refuse. 'I'm afraid of heights.'

'Ha!' He threw back his head and laughed. 'You're
a fraud, Marigold Scott! You spend the whole
morning telling me that you've got your act together,
then admit that you're afraid to go up in a perfectly
harmless hot-air balloon.'

'I never said I was brave,' she protested, and added
irrelevantly, 'and don't call me Marigold!'

'I won't, just as long as you agree to come in the
chase van, the next time I go up. You'll be safely
glued to the ground, and it may whet your appetite
enough to try going up. If nothing else, you should
know the roads around here well enough to keep my
crew reasonably close.'

'That's right!' she exclaimed, avoiding the need to

say whether or not she would do what he wanted. 'They never did find you.'

'I expect they've long since given up and gone back to the house and are waiting for me—or hoping that I'm not dead on the side of a mountain, which would mean the end of their jobs. I'd better get back and set their minds at ease. I'll send them down later to pick up the balloon. You know,' he added, pausing in the open doorway, 'this is going to be fun.'

'What is?'

'The contest between us. One of us is going to succeed in converting the other. Mark my words,' he finished, turning away, leaving her staring after his long, rangy figure until he disappeared around the corner of the house.

'Fun is the last thing I need!' Mari grumbled, going out to sit on the stepping-stone when she was sure Angus O'Neil was gone. She leaned back against the screen door and closed her eyes, resolving to put him out of her mind.

On this perfect morning in early June, the sun was bright against her closed lids; she could feel its warmth on her face, hear the occasional call of a bird and the lazy drone of a bumblebee. A feather-light breeze stirred her hair, bringing with it the heady scent of the lilacs still blooming by the edge of the woods. 'And what is so rare as a day in June?' she quoted dreamily, but her thoughts were already turning back to Angus O'Neil.

She wished she hadn't liked him so much. Liking a man could complicate her life, and she didn't think she could handle any complications. She'd avoided them for the last five years; she would be mad to let anyone complicate her life now! Still, there was nothing to say that Angus O'Neil *would* complicate her life, in spite of what he'd said about fun and contests and converting each other. If he had demons too—and she was pretty sure that he did—he wouldn't want complications any more than she did. One thing to be said for demons, she told herself with a brief, wistful smile; they were great inhibitors. Nothing like demons for clarifying things, for making sure that there were *no* complications at all!

So why not see a bit of Angus O'Neil? Provided, of course, that he didn't have a wife tucked away somewhere, Mari reminded herself. If he didn't, she wouldn't mind seeing more of this man who had, quite literally, dropped out of the sky. He was interesting and attractive and nice and . . .

In the far distance, she heard the faint sound of a truck labouring up the hill—Nate's truck, by the ragged sound of the silencer, but at this time of day it would be her sister Lily driving it. Nate would be haying, and Lily undoubtedly on her way into town, stopping first to see if Mari wanted anything. Thinking about Angus O'Neil would have to wait, Mari told herself, not moving, eyes still closed as the truck turned into her drive. She would think more about him at a later time—or not think about him at all. The choice was hers, and she would do as she pleased.

'Hello there!' called Lily, slamming the door of the truck and coming across the lawn to the step. 'You're lazy today.'

'I'm enjoying a rare day in June,' Mari explained, finally opening her eyes. 'No kids with you?'

'No. Nate's mother—bless her—has the little ones, and Junior is helping his dad. I'm off to pick up a part for the baler, and I just stopped to see if you——'

'—needed anything in town,' Mari finished for her,

and they both laughed. 'And for a cup of coffee?' she suggested, getting slowly to her feet and stretching widely.

'Of course. Damn! I'm too predictable, aren't I?'

'Nothing wrong with that. At least you're consistent. Come in,' Mari directed, pulling open the screen door. 'There's coffee on the stove. I forgot all about it, so it's bound to be too strong, but at least it's already hot.'

Inside the house, it was cool and dark after the bright sunlight outside. By the door, the two sisters paused for a moment, waiting for their eyes to adjust to the change.

'What's this?' Lily demanded as Mari started for the kitchen. 'It looks as though your social whirl started early today.'

'Oh, that.' Mari turned back to find Lily eyeing the remains of breakfast. 'Our mysterious millionaire dropped in, and I fed him. Do you know if he's married?'

'Bev Kelly says no. She went up there last week—bold as brass—to make, in her words, a social visit on his wife, and was told that—and I quote—Mr O'Neil doesn't *have* a wife. And why do you care?' Lily asked suspiciously. 'And how did he happen to drop in? And whatever made you feed him breakfast?'

'I care if he's married because I won't feed him breakfast again if he is. He happened to drop in because he was almost out of fuel and he landed his hot-air balloon in my meadow,' Mari explained, going into the kitchen for two mugs and what was left of the coffee. 'I fed him because it seemed like the neighbourly thing to do—I suppose you'll think I'm as bold as Bev, but he's really very nice.' She sat down at the table, pushing dirty plates aside and dividing the coffee between the two mugs. 'He's not at all mysterious, and definitely not what I'd call the millionaire type.'

'No?' asked Lily sceptically, picking up the champagne bottle, still three-quarters full, and reading the label. 'The Dom Perignon for breakfast was *your* idea?'

'Lord, I should cork it!' Mari jumped to her feet, working to force the cork back into the mouth of the bottle. 'Does Dom Perignon keep?'

'I haven't the slightest idea,' Lily told her, laughter and just a hint of concern reflected in her voice. 'You'd better ask your non-millionaire type. I bet he's an expert on Dom Perignon—and the plying of innocents with it first thing in the morning.'

'He didn't ply me, and I'm not exactly an innocent, Lily! I'm nearly thirty, and I lived in New York for six years.'

'You're still an innocent, in spite of all that,' Lily pronounced flatly. 'You've never said why you left New York in such a rush, just when things were going so well and you were about to get that big advancement, and I'm not asking you now. But *something* happened, Mari—something so bad that you walked away from a city you loved and a job you loved, a *life* you'd been loving madly. You just dumped everything and came back here to hide away on the side of a hill in pokey little Waterfield——'

'I love Waterfield,' Mari broke in to say. 'There's nothing wrong with this town! You love it too.'

'Of course I do, but I'm married.'

'And marriage makes everything right, is that it?' Mari asked, her voice shaded with unaccustomed bitterness.

'No, marriage doesn't make everything right,' Lily said with the hint of a smile, 'but it sure helps. The point, darling, is that I'm married, and I've got five kids. I've got roots here—a family, a life. You've got nothing!'

'I've got my business——'

'Don't go off on your business tangent again,' snapped Lily. 'You're using that damn business, *and* your role as the resident eccentric and hermit, for a reason—and I think that reason has to do with a man, or men in general.'

'Oh, men!' Mari made a disdainful face. 'You always come back to them.'

'I do, in your case. Why else did you settle in a town where the only eligible man is Dougie Henderson, the prize mama's boy of all time?'

'Because I don't care about that. I'm living the life that suits me,' Mari defended herself. 'I don't want to be married.'

'But you always did,' Lily reminded her. 'You were so enthusiastic about the idea, about finding someone so real and so right that together you'd make a whole. Mari, what happened to that?'

'I changed my mind.'

'Something changed your mind *for* you! Oh, Mari, I think about that—worry about it—and wonder sometimes what happened to you—if you got raped, or fell madly in love and then found out he was married, or fell madly in love with someone who walked out on you. Whatever happened, I'm afraid this Angus O'Neil may be what you ran away from New York to avoid.'

'He's not,' Mari countered quickly. 'I only met him this morning, but I can guarantee that he's not what I ran away from New York to avoid—not that I ran away from New York to avoid anything,' she qualified quickly. 'You've got that all wrong.'

'If you say so.' Lily sounded unconvinced, but she managed a smile of apology as she started towards the door. 'It's just that I care. Don't be angry with me.'

'Never,' Mari assured her, following Lily outside, watching as the truck drove away.

No, she wasn't angry, Mari told herself, settling again on the stepping-stone. She couldn't be angry, not when Lily—and the other members of the family too—meant so well. It was just that they worried about her too much, and always had. It came of being the baby of the family, Mari supposed, but they had all kept it up long after she'd stopped being a baby—or even a child.

This hovering and worrying and always wanting the best for her had been the reason why she had left college after her second year and moved to New York. Attending the university in Burlington, no more than thirty miles from home, had been no way to establish her independence; in New York, she had finally managed to feel like an adult. Coming home for the occasional visit had been an acceptable compromise—brief bouts as the subject of family concern punctuating long periods of self-sufficiency in the city.

It had been good while it lasted, Mari reflected, leaning forward, locking her arms around her knees and resting her head on them, and it had lasted until the day her world had blown up in her face. Then, with her life in fragments, she had seen the sparrow collide with the glass, and instantly she'd known that she had to come home. Instinctively, she'd realised that she needed the beauty and slower pace, the comfortable safety of home—but *not* her family's concern and worry about the new reality of her existence.

That was why, in the first moment of knowing she had to come home, she had made the decision that she would *never* tell her family, never let them know what she was facing. They had wondered, of course, and tactfully probed her decision, but she'd never been exposed to the full force of their wild conjecture until today, when Lily's reaction to Angus O'Neil's appearance had brought it all to the fore. Until today, Mari's resolute—and successful—determination to be independent had kept the worst of their concern at bay. And now, if a friendship with Angus O'Neil was going to start her family hovering again, she'd just have to keep away from the man, keep *him* away . . .

Damn. She sighed and lifted her head to find a dog standing not ten feet away. He was medium size, a nondescript black and tan, and of no discernible breed. He was also the most thoroughly wretched dog she had ever seen: hair matted, so thin that each rib showed clearly, his whole body seeming to droop. But, for all his pitiable appearance, it was the expression in his eyes which clutched at Mari's heart. He was frightened and lost and starving and desperate, and it all showed in his wary, hopeless, pleading eyes.

'You poor thing,' she whispered, and saw the infinitesimal lifting of his ears. 'Poor thing, poor thing,' she crooned, extending one hand very slowly. 'Come here, fellow. It's all right. That's right,' she added in the same careful whisper when he started to move towards her, walking stiffly, as though each step cost him too much.

'That's right,' she said again when he was close enough, but when she lifted her hand to pat him he flinched away. She dropped her hand, letting it rest outstretched on her knee, continued with soft, encouraging phrases until he finally dared come to her.

First he rested his chin against her hand, then moved a little close, then a little closer still—like the slowest of slow motion, she noticed—until finally the weight of him was resting against her legs. She patted him, scratched behind his ears, smoothed her hand back along his matted coat, and when she thought he trusted her enough she stood up and led him into the house.

Already, as she fed him what remained of breakfast's Canadian bacon, Mari knew he was hers. He had neither collar nor tag, not unusual in this small farming community, but no Waterfield dog was this thin, this uncared-for. No, her found dog had come a long way, perhaps from the other side of the Cold Hollow Mountains. Nor had he been treated well, she decided, seeing the way he cowered whenever she moved too quickly.

'Poor Found Dog,' she crooned, kneeling beside him when he had finished the scraps, stroking his matted coat again. 'I'll take better care of you than they did—whoever they are. You belong to me now. You're staying.'

At that, his eyes, which had been anxiously following her every word and movement, closed briefly, as though in assent, but he opened them again as soon as she stood up. When she went to sit down at her embroidery frame, he got stiffly to his feet and came to settle beside her.

By the end of that first day, Mari knew that something had changed. It wasn't just the dog—whose name was already becoming Founder—although she was forced to admit that she was enjoying the company of this black and tan creature who so literally dogged her steps. Instead, it was the whole day which had changed things—changed *her*, she was forced to admit. She'd awakened to the detached inevitability of thinking the moment had arrived, only to realise that something very different had come into her life. Perhaps her meeting with Angus O'Neil had made such an impression on her because his arrival had been so unorthodox, and because it had come on the heels of the other, darker moment. Whatever the reason, he had seemed important; there had been instant communication or rapport between them, and she was tempted to want it to continue.

'But that's not a good idea,' she explained to Founder when he followed her up the stairs to the loft at bedtime. 'I don't want to let anyone else into my life—you and Angus O'Neil in one day are too much,' she continued, still talking to the dog as she rummaged through the blanket chest until she found an old quilt to serve as his bed. 'And you're a much better idea than Angus O'Neil,' she assured him as she turned out the light and climbed into bed, Founder on his quilt on the floor beside her, so that she could reach down and give him a final pat. '*You* won't cause any complications, will you, boy? You're a much better idea,' she repeated as she finally turned and buried her head in the pillow. But it was Angus O'Neil—not Founder—who invaded her drifting thoughts until she was finally asleep.

It was just as well that she had chosen the dog over the man, she reflected more than once over the next few days. If she had harboured any ideas of seeing the man often, they were dashed the next morning when, a few minutes after Founder had grown restless and begun to whine, the helicopter pinwheeled lazily over the ridge.

Well, he's gone back to the rat-race, thought Mari,

resisting the urge to run out and watch as the helicopter headed south-west, towards Burlington and the airport. There was no telling when he would be back. Thus far, to her knowledge, O'Neil had owned his place for six months and had visited it exactly three times, each time for no more than a couple of days.

'We'll do fine on our own,' she told Founder, and they did. During the next three days, the dog prospered. A trip to the vet in the village resulted in some shots and a generally clear bill of health. A bath and a thorough grooming made him into a more presentable dog. More to Founder's liking, a judiciously mixed diet, including plenty of treats, had already begun to fill out the stark angles of his ribs.

For herself, Mari was deeply engrossed in a new design, a rainbow to be done in Romanian couching stitch—slow and tedious to do, but producing a beautifully textured effect. It was work to absorb her thoughts completely, and it did that—except in the evenings, when her day's work was done. Then, with Founder asleep at her feet, she spent endless hours with her sketching-pad, working on designs for hot-air balloons, trying to find colours and stitches to capture the magic that had floated over her house that rare morning in June.

On the fourth day, late in the afternoon, Founder grew restless again. When he began to whine, as he had the morning Angus O'Neil's helicopter had left, Mari looked at him in disgust. 'Don't tell me! Are you trying to prove how good your hearing is? And do you do this only for helicopters, or could it just be a sports car this time?'

It wasn't a sports car, and it was more than five minutes later before the helicopter sailed over the house, gradually dropping out of the sky as it made for the top of the ridge.

'Oh, you're good,' Mari told Founder, stooping to scratch the spot under his chin that mattered most. 'You're the best—my distant early warning system, should I decide that I need one. And I may,' she assured him while those bright, expectant eyes, braver now than they had been the day he'd come to her, stared back. 'Let's go out,' she suggested, straightening up, watching Founder jump when he heard the words he loved best. 'I feel like playing hard to get. Just in case that man does come visiting, he needs to know that I don't care that he's back. Maybe *I* need to know it, too,' she added, holding the door for Founder before going around to the shed to get out her trusty old ten-speed.

This was Founder's favourite outdoor sport, to race along beside the bike when she rode down the hill between her meadow and the Washers' pasture, past their place and the smooth field of fodder corn, sailing down into the stand of trees by the stream that ran beneath the faded paint and silvered boards of the old covered bridge. Once through the cool and shadowy shelter of the bridge, Mari had to gear down and labour to make the even steeper hill that twisted tightly up the other side. There wasn't much challenge for Founder in her slow speed, so he departed from the route, detouring around the occasional stone wall or clump of trees, slipping under fences to sniff out the unexpected intrigues of a summer country road.

Finally, at the top of the hill, they would stop together, both out of breath, staring back down the twisted road they had come up. Then Mari's gaze, at least, would follow the road back up the other hill until her eyes could make out her own place—white paint, green shutters, maples on the lawn, the lilacs still in bloom. Behind her house, the tangled skein of second growth climbed the ridge, ending with a raged edge of leaves against the sky. Beyond lay what had once been an old farmhouse, prettied up by a city family to be their summer place. When those strangers had lost interest and put it up for sale, it had stood empty for two years—until O'Neil had swooped down and claimed it, paying cash.

'And when do you suppose he became *O'Neil* to me?' Mari asked Founder now, balancing her toes lightly on the road, prepared to fly back down the hill. 'He was Angus O'Neil—all one word—and suddenly he's become *O'Neil*. I've never known an Angus, except Nate's Black Angus bull, and I can't bring myself to call a man by a bull's name. It's too much! I'll call him O'Neil when I see him—*if* I see him,' she called to the sky, pushing off, pedalling just a few times before gravity and momentum captured her again.

By the time she and Founder regained her little house—six miles and nearly half an hour later—the shadows cast by the maples had lengthened across the lawn to lie on the stepping-stone by the door, where O'Neil sat waiting for her. More angles today than before, she thought, following the line of his beaky nose and jutting chin, the way he rested long forearms on long thighs, elbows thrusting sideways, knees drawn up sharply. He's waiting for me, she told herself, wondering whether to be frightened or pleased.

CHAPTER TWO

'WHERE were you?' he asked, unfolding himself to remind her of just how tall and broadly built he was. 'I assumed you'd be home.'

'Never make assumptions about me,' she told him, swinging off the bike, taking a moment to tuck her knitted top back into the waistband of her jeans. 'I'm unpredictable.'

'Didn't you hear me coming?'

'God and his uncle heard you coming.' She stopped on the lawn, a few steps away, hands in her back pockets, returning his smile while she caught her breath. 'There's no way not to hear you coming.'

'And when you did, you rushed to get back,' he supplied, something in his expression waiting, watching to see if he would find what he wanted.

Mari shook her head. 'No. When I heard you, I rushed to get away—so you wouldn't think you can take me for granted.'

'Isn't it a little too soon for that?'

'It's a little too soon for a lot of things, O'Neil,' she retorted, moving past him to open the door for Founder.

'I didn't know you had a dog.' O'Neil came to stand in the kitchen doorway, watching while she drew fresh water for Founder's bowl and put down his food. 'He wasn't around the last time I was here.'

'That's right. He arrived later that day.'

'Two strays in one day, Marigold?' O'Neil enquired, his smile quizzical now, and she discovered

29

his ability to say at least as much with the lift of one eyebrow as with his words. 'For a rolling stone, you seem to be gathering a lot of moss.'

'Not yours! Founder's light years ahead of you.'

'Obviously. You've already given Founder his supper. He's spent the last four days with you—and the last four nights, I bet.'

'Slow down, O'Neil,' she warned, and he grinned again.

'Don't worry. I don't expect supper, or days and nights. Just a little dry Vermont humour and staunch independence.'

'Oh, no, now I'm *quaint*!'

'Well, you are, Mari. There's no getting around it, and I've spent the last four days listening to people say exactly what they *ought* to, to me. Can you blame me for wanting a little more substance?'

'Worse! I'm quaint, and you're the poor put-upon millionaire. You're turning us into clichés, O'Neil.'

'Not even I could do that,' he said with complete confidence, a kind of near-arrogance that was so unexpectedly attractive that it took her breath away. 'We're both too strong.'

'So long as you don't forget it. It's a two-way street——'

'—and we won't collide if we each keep to the right. Don't worry, Mari. I had you pegged from the start. We're two of a kind, the kind who always keep to the right. Which is enough of that kind of talk for one day. I only came to see if you wanted to come out tomorrow at dawn.'

'I'm not going up in your hot-air balloon!'

'I know,' he agreed cheerfully, detaching himself from the kitchen doorway, going back outside. 'You're going to chase, that's all. A quarter-past five, by my house,' he called over his shoulder, already out-side in the twilight. 'I trust you can find your own way up the hill.'

'And back down again—when I please.'

'That's right,' he agreed, in his eyes an expression of lazy approval. 'And don't accuse me of moving too fast, just because I came down here tonight. I wouldn't have needed to bother, if you had a tele-phone. Just think, Mari—if you'd put one in, you wouldn't have to see nearly as much of me, and it would be much more convenient for me.'

'Ha! Pigs will fly before I make things more con-venient for you!'

'That's my girl, Mari!' He smiled, unguarded and pleased. 'Five-fifteen,' he reminded her, and was gone.

Mari took Founder with her, the two of them stealthy shadows in the dark of pre-dawn, sensing their way up the twisted path through the second growth of the ridge. When they reached the top, the plateau where the helicopter landed, the darkness had been rent by a brilliant plume of flame.

'It's all right, boy,' Mari reassured Founder when he stopped, leaning doubtfully against her leg. 'It's a hot-air balloon, and the hot air has to come from somewhere.'

Closer to, the scene was like a strange tribal rite: three dark figures slowly dancing around the flame and the barely stirring form of the deity on the ground. Standing just beyond the circle with Founder beside her, Mari was caught by the magic of the moment. Even the engine powering the fan to blow heated air into the balloon had a slow, rhythmic, steady throb, like the sound of a chant.

'You're early,' O'Neil called when he finally noticed her, his long shadow detaching itself from the others to join her. 'It's going to be quite a while. There's a flask of coffee in the van. Help yourself.' His hand was briefly on her arm, steering her in that direction, then he was back to the dance again.

Mari watched, sipping black coffee, Founder leaning against her leg again. The balloon began to grow, coming alive in both form and colour as the dawn broke. Finally, as he climbed into the basket, O'Neil hurriedly introduced his two helpers.

'Savin and Rule,' she repeated for Founder's benefit as the two released the tether so that O'Neil and his towering rainbow of colour could lift away from the ground. It was not the gentle transition she had expected, but came in a rush, as though man and balloon were anxious to meet with the sky.

'Next time, you can come,' he shouted down, already moving down the field and higher. 'If you please.'

'Pigs will fly before *I* do, O'Neil!' she shouted back. He was still close enough for her to see his quick grin, but he was already alone, aloof, isolated and far away . . . in a world she knew nothing about, she reminded herself sharply, resolutely turning away.

Savin and Rule were waiting for her, two serious young men, clearly O'Neil's employees, not friends. Their attitude made it clear that they were being paid to be up before dawn, to have the van running and to see that she and Founder were in the rear seat. Once off and following O'Neil, they were busy with their maps and radio checks, discussing the obscure points of balloon flight and navigation. Mari definitely wasn't included in their activity, so she chose to ignore them as effectively as they ignored her. She kept her gaze on the bright ball of colour in the lightening sky, realising that it appeared to be moving more slowly now only because it was far above them.

Occasionally she heard O'Neil's voice, made metallic and cold by the radio: 'Space to base, you've got a left coming up . . . unless it's a dead end. Now, somehow . . . around or over this ridge . . . Any chance, do you think, that you'll find me by breakfast-time?'

In the end, it was Mari who knew where he was, on the south side of the small wooded mountain known as Cannon's Slope. 'Coming down in the trees,' Savin or Rule said to the other, and when they exchanged quick, worried glances Mari was forced to lean over the seat.

'No. There's an old gravel quarry half-way up—he's sure to have seen it.'

'I'm coming down in some kind of quarry,' O'Neil's voice broke in to confirm. 'Heaven knows how you'll get here . . .'

'Stop! Turn here,' Mari directed, forcing the men to take a narrow gravel drive between two pastures. 'There's a track up to the quarry.'

'There can't be,' the one with the map said flatly. 'No road shows here.'

'But there is.' She pointed the way through the trees. 'How else do you think they got the gravel out?' In the back seat, she gripped Founder's collar as the van bucked its way up the hill. Then, when she caught her first glimpse of the descending rainbow, she felt a rush of pure adrenalin.

The van arrived in the wide bowl of the quarry just as the balloon lost its last few feet and the basket began to drag. 'Oh, *yes!*' Mari cried, out and running, Founder beside her and barking, as enthusiastic as she. 'Ha! We made it, O'Neil,' she yelled, catching the edge of the basket even before the balloon began to subside. 'What *fun!*'

'Yes, and you're good, Marigold.' His blue gaze held hers while he swung out of the basket, while he peeled off his gloves and stuffed them into a pocket. 'Damn good.' His arm dropped on to her shoulders, pulling her into the line of his body, close enough for her to measure his slow, deep breaths against her own quicker ones. 'What in heaven't name is this place?' he demanded, turning a full circle with her against him, taking in the random collection of rusting hulks.

'We call it the elephants' graveyard. Junk cars just happen to find their way here, usually late at night. Aesthetically, it's less than pleasing——'

'Worse than that,' he corrected, now turning her to face him, the two of them oblivious to Savin and Rule as they worked to subdue the balloon. 'It's a good thing I didn't waste your first trip up with me on this hole.'

'Why?' she asked quickly, forgetting that she intended no first trip. 'I wouldn't care.'

'But I would. The first time we go up together, we're going to come down and have a picnic, while Savin and Rule—assuming they actually have a clue where we are, which I doubt—cool their heels until we're good and ready for them. Is that an idea that might please you?'

'Yes. No . . . It might . . . Damn!' She turned away from him to see that the two men were nearly done with the process of packing up the balloon. 'I wish I weren't so afraid.'

'Of me, or the balloon?'

'Both, I suppose.'

'There's no need to be, Mari.' She felt his arm on

her shoulders again, this time a light, impersonal touch. 'The balloon's safe enough; you've seen me land twice, and both times I've come down in one piece. And *I'm* no threat, believe me. I don't intend to be one; I don't want to be one. You're safe as houses with me, Marigold Scott.'

'Which *you* won't be, if you keep calling me that!'

'But that's part of the game—don't you see? We're two of a kind, and we like to play the same game. What's wrong with that, between friends?'

'Damn! When you put it that way——'

'You see, *Mari?*' he teased. 'It doesn't have to be hard.'

On the trip back, O'Neil took the wheel of the van, Founder claiming the front passenger window to crowd her close to O'Neil. Behind them, Savin and Rule were a silent presence, employees being paid to be driven back to their base. For O'Neil, the two other men didn't exist. He talked easily to Mari about the flight, the wind currents, the view. He made a few jokes, even teased her, ignoring her stiff and awkward replies as easily as he ignored Savin and Rule.

A selective and disciplined mind, she reflected, watching his hands on the wheel. He had ten times the discipline she had, ten times the control . . . and beautiful hands. They were large, long and slender, but surprisingly capable hands, the kind she would expect to find embracing the bow and strings of a violin, but looking absolutely right and at home resting lightly on the wheel.

'Breakfast on me today,' O'Neil announced, pulling into his drive, then turning to speak over his shoulder to Savin and Rule. 'Breakfast as soon as possible, and something for the dog.' Not waiting for a reply, he swept Mari and Founder into the house.

Mari had been inside once before, when it had been for sale and Lily had persuaded the agent, an old schoolfriend, to show them through. Mari could remember that visit well enough to see that the place really hadn't changed at all. The formal living-room held the same furniture and the same unlived-in air. Down three shallow steps, into what had been the carriage shed, she knew the closed door on the right opened into a large and decidedly masculine bedroom suite. Where O'Neil slept each night, she thought with a small shiver of unknown emotion, then decided to direct her attention to the three more shallow steps which took them into the converted old hay barn. This was a cavernous place of hand-hewn, silvered beams, lofts and balconies, an immense fieldstone fireplace and a wall of windows facing the field and the slow march of hills and mountains beyond.

'Haven't you changed anything?' asked Mari, looking around, remembering the casual rattan and cotton cushioned couches and chairs, the white wrought-iron and glass occasional tables, the long pine trestle table by one of the windows. 'It looks just the same.'

'It is, more or less. I put in better lighting.' He gestured upwards, and Mari saw the latest in track lighting, severely simple, high-tech black lamps mounted on the walls and cross-beams.

'Impressive. You can light up this place like a Christmas tree.'

'I often work late—plans and drawings.' He gestured again, and Mari noticed the one other addition to the room, a starkly modern work-table where an impressive computer shared space with a collection of cylindrical tubes.

'What do you do?'

'I'm an engineer. My company builds bridges and dams, irrigation systems, power plants, agricultural stations, desalinisation plants. We work in Third World countries, providing the locals with training along with the technology. The point, you see, is to make people self-sufficient,' he explained, dropping into one of the rattan chairs, absently scratching Founder's neck when the dog came to stand beside him. 'I won't do things *for* people, only *with* them, and it's got to be ecologically and economically sound. It's still a problem, this business of moving out of the old colonial mentality . . .'

He was off, his eyes far away, his voice fired with a kind of enthusiasm and intensity Mari had not heard before. Glory be! she thought, still listening without understanding the words, here's some real emotion, something that matters to O'Neil. But still the same selective and disciplined mind, she noted, repressing a smile as he continued talking. He was oblivious to the comings and goings of Savin and Rule, setting the table, bringing coffee, providing Founder with food and water.

'It's all changed, you see,' he was explaining when one of the men returned to serve their meal. 'When I started, I took the conventional route, went into these places and frequently raped the land, made enormous profits, of course . . . Then, like Saul on the road to Damascus, I suppose, I saw the light, realised that there had to be a better way, a *fairer* way to do business.'

Subliminally, at least, the presence of food had made an impression. Still talking, he got up to load first her plate, then his own, with pancakes and bacon, fried eggs and store-bought blueberry muffins. Frankly starving, Mari worked her way through the uninspired and heavy food; O'Neil left his untouched, although the quality seemed to have nothing to do with his apparent lack of appetite.

Once launched upon the subject of his work, he was like a man possessed, fired with the enthusiasm of a zealot. 'It's a matter of professional pride,' he explained at one point, 'to see that my firm produces the best possible designs, and a matter of personal concern that we're responsible about how we work with the people who hire us.' Long after Mari's plate was empty, he was still going, describing specific projects to illustrate his points.

'Have I lost you?' he demanded after one particularly technical detail, finally pausing to focus directly at her. When he did, he saw her empty plate and grinned apologetically. 'Lord, have I been talking that long? I must have bored you to tears.'

'Not at all. It's exciting to hear, exciting to see *you* excited.'

'I don't know if excited is the right word.' Belatedly, he picked up his fork, chewed reflectively on a mouthful of cold food, then set down the fork, a pained expression on his face. 'I don't suppose it was much good to begin with—neither of those two knows much about cooking—but it's even worse cold. Sorry I went on at such length. I try not to get carried away—which is one of my worst failings—but you're too good a listener. You didn't do anything to curb my enthusiasm for pre-stressed concrete and Third World development. I should concentrate more on the social niceties.'

'But you won't. You, O'Neil, are one of the most dissociated people I've ever met.'

'Am I?' he asked, the perplexity of his expression very real. 'I'm too wrapped up in my work—I'll grant you that, but how do you arrive at the conclusion that I'm dissociated?'

'All I had to do was take one look at this place. Except for the lighting and the work-table, you haven't changed a thing.'

'Just like a woman,' he grumbled. 'Did you expect me to redecorate, for heaven's sake?'

'No, but any normal person would have done something to make it his own—let a little personality show. And look at Savin and Rule,' she continued, warming to the subject. 'They've got about as much personality as two boards, and you hardly say a word to either of them.'

'Why should I? They're not friends. They work for me.'

'Exactly.' She propped her chin on her hand to stare across the table at him. 'And I bet you hired them *because* they don't have any personality. You go ballooning and let them chase you; you let them cook your meals—not very well, if this one's anything to go by—and you never give them a thought. You're willing to spend time with me, but you wouldn't be, if I began making demands—and don't think that's what's bothering me,' she hurried on when she saw him about to speak. 'It's not! You must know by now that I'm not going to make demands of you, and I certainly don't want you making them of me. That doesn't bother me, but it's all part of a pattern.

'Your problem, O'Neil, is that you're not *involved*,' she said sternly, 'except in pre-stressed concrete and Third World nations. You don't even *care*, except about nice safe, inanimate, global things. And I am *not* complaining,' she put in quickly, seeing him about to object. 'It's just that I wanted to get it straight—figure it out. So I'll know what I'm up against,' she finished abruptly.

'You're not up against anything, Mari.' He pushed back his chair and got up to prowl briefly round the room, finally coming to rest by the fieldstone fireplace, producing a thin cigar from a wooden box and making a careful production of lighting it. 'I thought—that first morning—that we enjoyed each other's company. I thought there was a degree of—well, friendship between us, which is not something I stumble across very often. You seemed *promising*. Lord knows, in your own way, you're at least as unorthodox as I, and I had nothing but friendship in mind. I made it clear—at least, I intended to—that I wasn't interested in more than that, and I *thought* you did the same.'

'I did.'

'Then what's to be up against?' he asked with a disarming grin.

'You, and your talk about contests and games. It's true: I don't want to get involved. I won't get involved—not with you, not with anyone. But I *do* happen to care about a lot of things more animate than pre-stressed concrete!'

'That's all right, I don't mind,' he assured her, prowling the room once more, trailed by a thin line of smoke. 'I never said we had to be exactly alike, that we *were* exactly alike. You may care about whomever you like—your family, Founder, Savin and Rule . . .'

'Just don't care about you,' Mari put in calmly.

'Exactly!'

'I don't want to,' she explained honestly, 'and it's not as though there's any reason to think that I *will* . . . but it's a risk *I* take and you don't.'

'Don't *worry* so, Mari! It's not really that much of a risk. I won't be here often—I'm elusive as hell most of the time—and believe me, I can spot *care* at a distance. If I see you beginning to slip, I'll remember to call you Marigold, or go off to check on a project in Mozambique. How are you going to care about someone that far away?'

'You make it sound so simple . . .'

'It *is* simple.' He paused to stub out his cigar, then came across to the table, placing his palms on the surface to bend down, until his face was level with hers. 'You're making too much of it all. You've got roots in this place, and I haven't. You want roots and I don't—that's all clear enough. What's the harm, then, if once in a while I drift in and out and we spend a few amusing hours together?'

'I haven't got an answer to that.'

'Because there isn't one,' he said on a soft note of triumph.

Mari didn't see him again that day, or the next; he was wise enough to give her some space, or perhaps he was too busy to bother with her, she reminded herself. On the third day, he arrived just before dusk, at the end of a heavy and humid day.

'May I come in?' he called from the stepping-stone, standing there with his hands dug deep into the pockets of the usual faded jeans, a white knit shirt emphasising both the depth of his tan and the breadth of his shoulders. 'I was going to ask you to go up with me, but the air's too dead. We'd get nowhere.'

'That sounds like the ideal balloon ride,' she observed, getting up from her embroidery frame, padding barefoot across to the door. 'And yes, you may stay,' she told him, seeing the careful reserve in his eyes—and liking him better for it, 'but I'll come outside instead, on the off chance that it's cooler outside.'

'It's worth a try, I suppose, although you look cool as it is.' He eyed her floating white muslin shift with its wide set-in sleeves and pale blue-green embroidery at the neck. 'That's nice. Is it something you did?'

'Just about everything I own is something I did,' she explained, sitting down on the doorstep and planting her feet in the grass, watching as he lowered himself down beside her. 'I always make first models to fit myself, so I've got an extensive wardrobe.'

'All originals from Marigold, Inc. Aren't you lucky?' he teased. 'I can think of a number of places in New York where you could appear in that dress and have fashion-plates clamouring to know the name of your designer.'

'Thank you.' She inclined her head, caught a little off balance by the clear admiration in his tone. 'For that, I'll reward you with supper—if you like, and if you haven't already eaten.'

'Why do you think I came down?' he asked with his off-centre grin. 'I've got a craving for home cooking tonight.'

'You set me up! You rigged this whole thing!'

'That's right, Marigold,' he agreed unrepentantly, getting up to follow her into the kitchen where she threw together cold roast chicken and salad greens, spring water with fresh lime.

They ate on the stepping-stone, balancing their plates on their knees, feeding occasional scraps to Founder as the shadows lengthened and the red ball of the sun finally dropped behind the mountains. They talked, about nothing much in particular—his work and hers, city things and country things, books they had read, things they enjoyed.

'Storms,' Mari contributed in response to the first

dull rumble of thunder. 'I always sit here to watch when one comes in from the west. I can track the lightning as it comes closer, and it makes a wonderful show. I love it!'

'Because you're as wild and free as the storm.'

In the darkness, she heard the smile in his voice, could almost feel it against her skin. Suddenly, unaccountably, she wanted more than almost. She wanted O'Neil to touch her, to take her hand in his large one, or to put his arm around her shoulders as he had after the balloon flight. Do *something*, O'Neil! she prompted silently, but he didn't. Instead, he just sat, the line of her body not three inches from hers, the two of them wordlessly watching the storm's approach until it was nearly upon them.

'Well, I'd better go back, if I don't want to get struck by lightning,' he announced, getting up, extending his hand to help her to her feet. 'Are you feeling better about us, after this evening?'

'Yes.' Now! she urged, her hand still held captive in his. They were standing so close, and in the heavy night air the scent of him was a disturbing tangle of astringently clean aftershave, cigar smoke and something disconcertingly *male*. Honest sweat, she thought it was—a fine filming of salt on his skin, and she wanted to touch it and taste it and . . . Do *something*, O'Neil!

'Thanks for your hospitality.'

'It was nothing.' And it's going to stay nothing, damn you! 'What?' she asked distractedly when she realised he had spoken again.

'I asked what you'd do if I kissed you.'

'Kiss you back,' she practically snapped, and a conveniently timed bolt of lightning split the sky, turning night to an instant of day, allowing her to see the wise laughter in his eyes. 'You *knew* I'd say that!'

'No . . . I take nothing for granted with you,' he murmured, his lips already teasing lightly at hers. 'I'm never quite sure . . .'

But she *was*, as the moment built and her lips parted to welcome the possession of his. Oh, *yes*! she thought when he drew her close. This was a small piece of heaven—to want and to know herself wanted, to feel the intensity of his need meeting hers . . .

'I think we've both been struck by lightning,' he said at last, sounding every bit as unsteady, as shaken, as she felt. 'And after something like that, I think it's time for a little sober reflection.' Instantly he released her, turning away into the darkness of the storm.

'He's deep,' Mari told Founder two days later, when there had been no sign of O'Neil. 'He's deep and clever . . . and what does he *do* up there all the time?'

It was evening, and she was still labouring over her Romanian couching stitches, keeping her hands busy by carefully working the stitches in indigo silk. 'I suppose he does plans for dams and bridges and desalinisation plants, and I'd love to watch him work,' she told Founder, imagining O'Neil's angular length bent over the work-table, his long, beautifully tapered fingers using—no, caressing a protractor or compass, making fine, graceful lines across a virgin sheet of paper. 'You know,' she continued to Founder, setting down her needle and getting up to stare out of the window, 'we do the same thing—not you and me, but me and O'Neil. We see things—designs and shapes and relationships—in our minds, then we have to transfer them to paper. The only difference between us, as far as I can tell, is that he doesn't believe in taking breaks. Or else he's still being deep and clever,' she finished, forcing herself to turn away from the window and go back to the needle and thread which suddenly seemed like an extreme form of penance. 'And still playing games with my head—damn him to hell!' she added, with such vehemence that Founder stirred uneasily and came to lean close to her leg.

Whatever anger she'd felt—and it really hadn't been anger, but something more like discontent or confusion—vanished when he appeared in the third day's late afternoon.

'It's a perfect day to go up,' he announced from the doorstep, 'or to stay on the ground, if you're still not convinced.'

'I'll go up,' she said almost crossly. 'It's one of life's little adventures, and I suppose I should cram in as many of them as I can.' Besides, she wanted to be near him, be *with* him, and her fear of the sky was no longer as great as her wanting. And if being with him meant dangling from a rainbow balloon, with nothing but a small wicker basket between her and the earth—well, she would just have to accept that as the price to be paid. 'I'll go, but I'm going to be scared.'

'No, you won't. You'll love every minute.'

'How did you know I wouldn't be scared?' Mari demanded when the flight was history and their descent accomplished. The remains of their picnic meal, eaten in a high meadow somewhere near Johnson, had been packed away, and the last of the light had faded, giving the night to the stars.

She had left her fear on the ground, in the fractional moment when the tether had been released and the balloon had started its lift towards the sky. She had leaned over the edge of the basket, watching Savin and Rule and the van, O'Neil's house, then her own, all growing smaller, all being left on the ground—with her fear.

The fields had been green and golden in the slanting rays of the sun, the small centre of town a child's perfect model. The roads, she discovered, had a wilful logic of their own, following the gentler slopes of the hills, avoiding the steeper ones as they found their way from one point to the next. It was the world as she had never seen it before, the world without its imperfections, a world of form and sweep and infinite marks of small beauty. They crossed above very slowly, far more slowly than she expected, so there was plenty of time to see and absorb everything she saw. Around them was silence without distraction, only the occasional sound of the burner—that dull roar which came when O'Neil required more lift.

'This is *heaven*,' she told him once, turning away from her view only long enough to grip both his arms, given an instant to glimpse the laughter and understanding in his eyes.

Now, in the breeze-filled night, still on a high that had nothing to do with the food and champagne they had shared, she lay back on the blanket, arms crossed behind her head, and stared up at O'Neil's long dark shadow. 'How did you know I'd love it?'

'Because I know you.' In the darkness, he lit a cigar and there was a moment when the lighter flared and she saw his face clearly, its sharp planes and thrusting chin, the aliveness of his eyes and the fine network of wind and laughter-wrought lines. 'You're one to appreciate that kind of freedom.'

'Oh, yes,' she agreed, her voice dreamy, 'and the beauty. Funny——' he was still sitting beside her, but he'd leaned back, and now she had to tip her head to find his shadowy profile '—but I wouldn't have thought beauty mattered to you, yet that's got to be a part of it.'

'Of course.' He nodded, and now she knew he was smiling. 'There's more to me than pre-stressed concrete.'

'I wouldn't have thought so. You're an intimidating engineer. I didn't think I'd have anything in common with someone like you.' There was, of course, that vision she'd had of the way they both worked to create their designs, something better left unsaid. 'O'Neil,' she began again, 'do you remember that morning when I analysed you about not caring or getting involved?'

'Vividly.'

'Well, I almost used your ballooning as one more example of your detachment. I mean—what could be more detached than floating away in a hot-air balloon? It made a neat bit of symbolism, but I was wrong,' she explained, watching as a nearly full moon began to break free of the trees on the far side of the meadow. 'It's really incredibly involved—being up there, seeing the world so clearly.'

'True.' He tossed away his cigar, easing his length down next to her, lying on his side, his head supported by the angle of one arm, 'but tonight I was more involved with you—with watching your reactions, seeing your face, making sure that you liked it.'

'Well, I did,' she acknowledged absently, watching his face now, studying the contrast of moonlight and shadow and the tricks played with is features. 'I'm a convert, O'Neil.'

'To what?' he asked, smiling, his free hand beginning to toy with her hair, smoothing errant curls. 'To me, or hot-air ballooning?'

'Definitely hot-air ballooning, but I'm still not sure about you.'

'Why not?'

'Because I don't want any complications.'

'Fine. I don't want them, either.' He leaned closer, bending his head, touching his lips to her temple. 'Mari, there's no need to worry.'

'Yes, there is.' She lay very still, knowing she should turn her head away from the brief kisses he was scattering across her face, wishing she could be as detached about *this* kind of thing as he obviously was. 'O'Neil, this is a complication . . .'

'No.' Gently, he kissed her eyelids closed, then touched his lips lightly to hers. 'Not a complication, Mari,' he murmured, each word a small, piercing kiss. 'This is a pleasure.'

'That, too,' she agreed reluctantly, trying to gather her scattering thoughts. What he was doing felt so good, so right . . . It was, after all, what she had been wanting these last three days—but was it *wise*? Damn! She should have spent the last few days thinking—not wanting. Now the time for thinking was past. O'Neil —and her own weakness—were too much; she could feel herself slipping into a world where nothing seemed to matter, except his kiss, his scent, his taste . . .

'That's right,' he breathed when her lips parted to his. 'That's right, love . . . Yes!' he encouraged, an odd note of triumph in his voice when her hands moved to his shoulders.

Now his mouth closed over hers with reckless, compelling abandon, and she discovered that she could actually feel his need. It was there, a palpable force in the hard-corded muscles beneath her touch, in the unevenness of his breathing, in the insistent demand of his kiss. She hadn't known—hadn't realised—her power, and the knowledge that she could so profoundly affect him was her final undoing. His need for her, she discovered, was searing her soul, destroying the last vestiges of her control.

Mindlessly, her fingers tangled themselves in his thick hair, urging him closer while her body began to stir, arching towards the hard lines of his. 'O'Neil,' she whispered when his lips finally left hers, a wealth of confession in that one unsteady word.

'Sweet Mari,' he murmured, pulling away just a bit, his gaze holding hers while one hand touched her face, then the slender column of her throat. 'This is better . . . more . . . Isn't it, love?'

Better or more than what, she had no idea, but that didn't matter now. She nodded, transfixed, staring up at him, memorising his face and his eyes and the way the breeze stirred the careless slant of hair across his forehead. 'I didn't know,' she confessed, her breath catching when his long, clever fingers began to trace the careful line of embroidery that edged the neckline of her dress.

'Didn't know what?' he quizzed while his fingers continued their teasing—moving down across the swell of one breast, pausing briefly where the embroidery ended, then slowly, with maddening deliberation, beginning to move up the other side. 'What didn't you know?'

'About this . . . How good . . .' She sighed, fighting for some coherence, some defence against the sensuous game he was playing. 'O'Neil,' she breathed, her body aching for something more than just the fiery friction of his touch, 'what are you doing to me?'

'Pleasing you,' he explained with an abstracted smile, watching her face as he slipped his hand beneath the fabric of her dress to caress the soft swell of her breast. 'Prolonging the moment,' he continued, his voice begining to thicken, working with careful precision to dispatch the front closings of her dress, to sweep it aside. 'No, don't,' he commanded, catching her hands when she instinctively moved to cover her nakedness. 'Beautiful Mari, let me look at you.'

'No, please don't,' she whispered, desire suddenly tempered by caution. 'We've gone too far.'

'You're wrong,' he told her, one clever finger tracing the curve of her breast. 'We haven't gone far enough.'

'O'Neil, stop,' she pleaded. 'We can't *do* this!'

'Why not?' he asked absently, his lips busy exploring her face.

'Because——' she cast wildly for some plausible reason '—because Savin and Rule are waiting for us.'

'They don't matter.' He drew back slightly, staring down at her with a puzzled expression. 'Don't worry, Mari, they won't bother us.'

'That's not the *point*! Anyway, how do you know that?' she demanded, scrambling away from him, drawing her dress back around her and beginning to search for the fastenings. 'O'Neil, I just can't *do* it—make love and then stroll down the hill and ride home with them as though nothing has happened. That's *bizarre*—possibly even obscene!'

'I'd have called it practical and convenient,' he suggested drily, studying her face with a quizzical smile. 'What's the matter, love? Is it really Savin and Rule, or are you having second thoughts about what was beginning to happen between us just now?'

'Of course it's Savin and Rule,' she snapped, thanking heaven that she had thought of them in time. 'I just can't do it here, with them waiting . . .' Her hands moved in mute appeal. 'Can't you understand?'

'I must confess that the finer points escape me,' he observed, his tone still dry, but shaded with a little more reserve, as though he sensed her greater doubts. 'Correct me if I'm wrong, but you seemed—for a while, anyway—to want this as much as I do.'

'I did. I do,' she corrected quickly, feeling cornered, no longer certain *what* she wanted, needing time to think . . . But she didn't have time, she realised, sensing his withdrawal, the cool immobility of the way he was watching her. 'O'Neil,' she began again, afraid she might lose him completely over this, trying to buy herself some time, 'can't we go back to my place? You could send them home, and then we'd be alone . . .'

'So we would,' he agreed, an odd inflection in his voice, his unreadable smile caught by the moonlight. 'Is that what you want?'

'Yes.' The lie hung in the air between them while she tried not to shy away from his gaze.

'Then what are we waiting for?'

CHAPTER THREE

THERE should have been plenty of time to think during the ride back in the van. In fact, there *was* plenty of time; they had floated further than Mari had realised, so they were nearly an hour on the twisting country roads. But she was past thinking. The enormity of what she'd done—what she'd promised, or at least let O'Neil believe—weighed too heavily to her to permit coherent thought. When they got out of the van in front of her house, she was no closer to knowing what she wanted to do than she had been in that moonlit meadow.

'There. That's the end of Savin and Rule.' O'Neil stood by the edge of the road, watching until the van's tail-lights had disappeared from view. 'Alone at last, Mari.'

'Yes.' The word sounded stiff and awkward; she *felt* stiff and awkward as she walked to the door and opened it. 'Oh, no—Founder!' she shrieked as he erupted through the door, leaping and prancing, his body twisting in the air as he bounced from her to O'Neil and back. 'Poor boy! I forgot all about him,' she explained unnecessarily to O'Neil. 'He'll have to go out and be fed. Fresh water . . .'

O'Neil watched, a tall, silent figure, impassive, unknown, while she tended to Founder, waited patiently until she finally turned to face him. 'O'Neil,' she began uneasily, 'I don't know what to say.'

'Yes. I could tell.' His smile, when it finally did appear, lay somewhere between bleak and knowing.

'Second thoughts after all, Mari?'

'I suppose so,' she admitted, nervously threading her fingers together, staring down at them because she was afraid to meet his gaze. 'It's no excuse, and it might have been better if I'd just let it happen. At least,' she added in a rush of undiplomatic candour, 'we'd have had it over and done with.'

'Mari, that's no way to look at making love.'

'Yes. I know.' Ha! What did she know? she wondered unhappily, running her hands through her curls, wandering into the living-room to stand by her embroidery frame. Why did I ever meet him? she asked herself. Why didn't I just stay here setting stitches, and let this particular life experience pass me by? This tangle wasn't a part of the demons; this was reality, although she supposed she could blame the demons for the fact that she'd avoided this particular tangle for so long. 'O'Neil.' She drew a deep breath and took the plunge. 'I don't think we should make love. I don't think it's a very good idea.'

'I see.' Suddenly, he was standing directly behind her; he had moved so quietly—thanks to his sneakers, she supposed—that she hadn't known he had crossed the room until he spoke. 'Do you mind telling me why?'

'Because it would mean too much to me.'

'It needn't,' he rebutted flatly, not arguing with her, but merely stating a fact. 'We're two consenting adults, after all, and making love is simply another way of enjoying each other's company. When we talk, does that mean too much to you?'

'No,' she forced herself to admit, knowing full well where he was heading.

'And did it mean too much to you to go up in the balloon this evening?'

'No.'

'Then why will making love mean too much to you?'

'Because! You should have been a lawyer, reducing people to absolute mush on the witness stand. I'm a *virgin*,' she snapped, whirling around to face him, forcing herself to look up and meet his gaze. 'I'm a twenty-nine-year-old virgin. I've never made love before!'

To his credit, his expression betrayed neither amusement nor pity. Instead—and she knew she would always feel grateful to him for this—he merely pointed out, 'You'd never been up in a balloon before either.'

'It's *not* the same thing!'

'But closer than you think, love.' His smile was reflective, almost mellow. 'They're both incredible highs—no pun intended—and if the two people involved have the same feelings about it, both are grand ways to share things that can't otherwise be expressed. We have the same feelings about being in the air; you *know* we shared something up there. It will be very much the same when we make love.'

'We're not going to make love!' Mari took an instinctive step backwards and found herself trapped against her embroidery frame. 'If we did, you'd be the first, and then you'd be *special*!'

'No.' Suddenly his voice—his whole bearing—was dispassionately uninvolved, all pre-stressed concrete, she thought with an insight just this side of hysteria. 'I won't let that happen.'

'You won't have any choice, O'Neil! You won't have any control over how *I* feel! And I don't want to feel anything special for you—for anyone,' she wailed, feeling trapped. 'I don't *need* complications like that!'

'Complications again,' he observed, now smiling at her, reaching out to her with the warmth of his understanding. 'You worry too much about them, but there won't be any with me.' Still holding her captive against her embroidery frame, he placed his hands on her shoulders, watching her face, holding her gaze. 'I won't let there be any. I accept the fact that, since I'll be your first lover, you may have some special feeling towards me—at least at the start. I expect that's quite natural, but the feeling will pass, and then making love will be just one more pleasant thing we can share. If enjoying each other's company and going up in the balloon don't make me special, then making love won't either.'

'But what if it does?' she whispered, half mesmerised by his voice and his touch and his deep blue-black gaze. It would be so easy to listen to him and believe! A part of her wanted to, was battling fiercely with the instinct for self-preservation which had been guiding her actions for the last five years. But that instinct was what had kept her life together; she couldn't abandon it now! 'Or what—and maybe I'm flattering myself—but what if you begin to get involved with me? I mean, that would be just as bad—just as much of a complication. What happens if *I* begin to matter to *you*?'

'You won't,' he answered, his voice calm and curiously empty. 'I like you; I have a certain regard for you, but I won't let you matter to me. Mari, I was married once, many years ago. *She*—my wife—mattered to me, but she died, and I'm not about to let anyone else get that close.'

So that was why . . . 'I'm sorry, O'Neil.'

'You don't need to be. It's over now, but I've no desire to go through that again—that's why you'll never matter to me. If I found you beginning to—if I thought there were any chance that you might—I'd walk away, never see you again. It's as simple as that.'

Is it? she wondered. Was anything ever going to be simple between them again? 'But what if it begins to be not as simple for me?' she asked at last. 'If I tell you to go, will you do it?'

'Yes.'

He sounded so sure, and she envied him his certainty, but then he'd had more years in which to perfect his detachment. Besides, he was black and white, while she was shades of grey—and there the danger lay. And yet . . . 'Well, I suppose I can't ask for more than that,' she decided, almost against her will, poised on the edge of telling him to go right now. That, she knew, would be the safe course to take, but she lacked the courage to be safe. But still . . . 'O'Neil? Would you mind if we didn't see each other for at least a few days?'

'Of course not. I was going to suggest it myself,' he told her, the emptiness beginning to leave his voice, being replaced by a tone of amusement. 'I'd planned to leave tomorrow, anyway. I'll be gone about a week.'

'Good.'

'That's the spirit, Mari! You're already getting back in stride. You'll see. This really isn't going to be as hard as you think. In fact, you might even say that the two of us are made for each other—we're both so clear about what we don't want.' Gently, his lips touched her cheek, lingered there for a moment before he stepped back. 'Goodnight, Mari, and don't worry. Nothing will change.'

'Goodnight, O'Neil,' she whispered, waiting until he was gone. Then she closed her eyes against the unexpected threat of tears, knowing that everything had already changed.

'So—what's new between you and our resident millionaire?' asked Lily over coffee the next morning, adopting a deceptively casual air.

'He's no longer resident. Surely you heard?' Mari pointed out drily. The helicopter had launched itself into the air just after dawn; she was pretty sure that she and Founder weren't the only ones the sound had awakened. 'The whole town can hear when he comes and goes.'

'And when is he coming back next?'

'I have no idea,' Mari lied baldly. 'He doesn't confide in me.'

'No?' Lily's expression managed to combine scepticism and concern. 'You're spending an awful lot of time with him, from what I hear—breakfast and dinner, and flying around with him in that balloon. Everyone in town is talking about the two of you.'

'They would,' Mari observed grimly.

'Well, why not?' Lily demanded. 'You're one of us, and he's not. Frankly, I don't like the idea of your mad millionaire and his helicopters and hot-air balloons.'

'There's only one of each, he is not mad, and I don't think it's fair to call him a millionaire,' Mari rebutted, amused to discover that Lily was accomplishing quite the reverse of what she wanted. Hearing Lily's doubts only made Mari ignore her own to defend him. 'He works hard for a living, you know. He's an engineer, and his company builds things in Third World countries. It's a serious business.'

'Now you're taking his side,' Lily fretted, 'which means that it's serious between the two of you.'

'It's *not*,' Mari corrected just a little too quickly,

too sharply. 'It's just friendship, the kind I haven't had since I moved back here. I knew a lot of men like O'Neil when I lived in New York. We've got things in common to talk about, and we do a little verbal sparring, but that's all.' Well, nearly all, she amended, her thoughts skittering away from the memory of what had happened last evening. 'Look,' she continued, trying to reassure both herself and Lily, 'did it ever occur to you that I might like to just talk to a man? That I might enjoy having one who's just a *friend*? That's all it is—just friendship. Nothing serious!'

Upon reflection, Mari decided that what she'd told Lily was reasonably close to the truth—at least, close to the truth as Mari had known it before last evening had happened. That had made things a little more complicated, but she didn't think she needed to worry. If things did begin to get serious, she could trust O'Neil to keep his promise and walk away, never see her again.

Which wasn't what she wanted, she acknowledged with painful honesty. She wanted to see more of O'Neil, but on the old, easy footing they had had before last night. She wanted him without strings attached, wanted him the way she'd described it to Lily. And it just might be possible, she concluded optimistically. If anyone could pull it off, O'Neil could. He was so much stronger and surer—more ruthless—than she; surely she could trust him to keep the line between them clearly drawn?

At least she could *hope*, she told herself with a nervous little smile, not noticing—much less reflecting upon—the fact that it had been five years since she had permitted herself to entertain any possibility of hope.

*   *   *

The next few days held fair, so Mari used her bike to make a circuit of her sewing ladies. With Founder now for company, she went round to visit one or two each day, dropping off new work, picking up what had been completed, discussing what was in progress. These had always been friendly, informal visits, a nice mix of business and gentle town gossip; the only difference this time was that Mari found herself to be the subject of the gossip. All the ladies seemed to know precisely how many times she had seen O'Neil and most of them had caught at least a quick glimpse of her as she'd floated over the town with him.

'So exciting that must have been,' Lillian Downey observed after she and Mari had discussed how the stitches should be set for the new rainbow design. 'You must have been thrilled to be up there, and I suppose Mr O'Neil must be a charming man. Just make sure that he doesn't charm you *too* much!'

'A big city man,' was Maida Peterson's less benign assessment. 'I bet he's all glitz and glitter, so you'd better be careful, Mari. He's trouble—you'll see.'

'But what does he really want?' Edna Coutre wondered darkly. 'Most men want only one thing, and I doubt that he's any different. Hold out for marriage, dear. That's the only way.'

'You see, Founder? They've got it all figured out,' Mari told the dog when the visits were done, when they had gained the last hill and were lazing in the shade of the maple nearest the road. 'Lily would be thrilled to know that so many people are of her opinion! He's trouble, and I'd better be sure that he doesn't charm me too much. Lord knows, Edna's right—he *is* after only one thing, but I don't want to hold out for marriage! I am not the marrying kind—and that's final.' She sat up to scratch

Founder's favourite place, under his chin. 'I'm not even the kind to take in a dog, you know,' she continued after a minute. 'I was doing very nicely, thank you, before the two of you came along—and on the same day!—to complicate things.'

Then, because she didn't like the direction her thoughts were taking, she went to check the mail. There were two bills, four advertising circulars, and a postcard. Its picture was of a crowded bazaar—very Third World, Mari saw, her heart suddenly beating fast. When she turned the card over, it was to see boldly precise printing done with fine black ink in the style of calligraphy without the embellishments. This was a master's hand, she decided, the bills and junk mail tucked forgotten under one arm; this was a master's hand and a master eye for line and form. So strong was the visual impact that it was a while before she even bothered to read what O'Neil had written: 'Come with me some time,' he'd told her, taking entirely too much for granted. 'I'd never noticed before, but the markets are full of embroidery. You ought to see it for yourself—it might give you new ideas. I should be back about the time this comes. O'Neil.'

In fact, he came the next day. As always, Founder gave the first warning, beginning to whine and pace five minutes before Mari heard the first small sounds of the helicopter.

'I swear I don't know how you do it,' she told him, rewarding him with a piece of cheese, 'but I'm glad you can. It gives me time to prepare myself for the idea of facing him.'

But nothing could really prepare her, she discovered when O'Neil appeared at her door not an hour later. 'I took time for a shower—you wouldn't have wanted me otherwise,' he announced, and once she had let him in he filled her small living-room with a presence larger and more vital than she'd remembered. Dressed in his usual uniform of faded jeans and knit shirt, he was freshly shaven, his hair still damp from his shower. He is splendid! she thought, standing motionless by the door, waiting to see if he would kiss her.

He didn't. Instead, he began to prowl restlessly round the room, pausing once to study the work in progress on her embroidery frame, again to notice his postcard on the table. His tan had grown several shades darker; he was brown now, with the result that his eyes seemed a lighter shade of blue. And somehow set a little more deeply, she decided, studying him more closely. There was an edginess about him, a fine-honed quality, as though he had lost weight or been pushing himself too hard.

'You look tired.'

'Stiff,' he corrected with brief economy. 'Too many hours in too many planes. Do you have any idea how many times I had to change planes between here and Lagos?'

'None. I don't even know where Lagos is.'

'Nigeria. That's where I was last,' he explained absently, still in motion, circling the room like a caged bear. 'Could I have a cup of coffee?' he asked.

'You don't need coffee, O'Neil. You may have spring water or herb tea.'

'Spring water, then. Deliver me from herb tea,' he grumbled, his expression pained. 'Just my luck to come racing back from Africa to be with a girl who won't even give me a cup of coffee! I've gotten myself mixed up with a damned hippie. Is that home-made bread?' he demanded when, having followed her into the kitchen, he saw the loaf.

'Made yesterday by one of my sewing ladies. Are you hungry?' she asked, and was rewarded by a grin.

There was something deeply satisfying about feeding a hungry man good food, she reflected when he'd settled on the couch with his plate and glass. She took her place at her embroidery frame, working easy, undemanding stitches, watching him with half an eye as he made short work of the two thick sandwiches she had made for him. This wasn't the same as making a meal for the two of them to share. This was taking a little care of O'Neil, who had obviously been working hard and travelling long. She was looking after him, she decided, that thought giving her a feeling of contentment which lasted only until the food was gone and he leaned back against the cushions of the couch.

'Lord, that tasted good,' he told her. 'I take back everything I said about you being a hippie. You're definitely worth racing back to.'

'Careful, O'Neil,' she cautioned—cautioning both of them, she supposed, reminding them both that they shouldn't let themselves get too *comfortable*. Which he was doing, she saw, watching as he stretched out his long legs, now totally at ease—at *home*!—in her little living-room. 'You're not supposed to feel that way, not if you want this to be a casual friendship.'

'Not just a friendship, Mari,' he objected with a lazy smile. 'Remember? There's going to be more to it than that.'

'So *you* say, but I think you're wrong!' Angrily, she jabbed her needle through the linen, wishing he didn't sound quite so sure of himself, wishing he weren't sprawled on her couch with quite such indolent grace. 'You're crowding me, O'Neil!'

'Would you feel that way, I wonder, if I left you alone—and guessing—for a few days? With any luck at all, that might make you miss me just a bit. I guarantee that I'd be missing you—your tart tongue and your prickly sense of what's right and wrong. I *did* miss them, while I was gone.'

'Damn it, O'Neil! I don't want you missing me, and I certainly don't want to be missing you!'

'But that's part of the fun, Mari,' he explained complacently. 'That's part of the chase, and I've reached a point in my life where the chase means nearly as much as what comes after. Of course . . . what comes after will be very pleasant,' he added, the hint of a smile playing at the corners of his mouth. 'I realise you can't know that yet, given your refreshing lack of experience——'

'O'Neil——' she interrupted in a strangled tone.

'—but we'll enjoy ourselves,' he finished, an easy gesture dismissing her attempted protest. 'Believe me, love, it's going to be worth the wait.'

'I wish you wouldn't keep talking that way,' she said distractedly, staring in dismay at the crazy mess of stitches she had just put into the linen. 'You make it sound so cold-blooded, which is the way it should be, given the way we don't want to feel . . . but it's embarrassing. What you want—well, I'm not ready for it. I'm not sure I'll *ever* be ready!'

'I know.' The teasing note was suddenly gone from his voice, replaced by understanding. Risking a quick look, she found him holding out his hand to her. 'Mari, come here.'

'No!'

'Yes, love. You can't always hide behind that embroidery frame of yours. It's time for you to learn that being close won't automatically lead to that final step that frightens you. Mari,' he said again, softly, but with compelling force, 'come and be with me.'

She had no choice. It was, after all, not only what she feared, but what she wanted—to be close to him, to draw upon his strength and his assurance, to feel his arms around her, dissolving five long years of loneliness and fear.

'Don't worry, love,' he told her when she joined him, drawing her into his arms until her body was resting against the long line of his. 'There's nothing wrong with being close.'

'But it confuses me,' she complained half-heartedly, leaning her head on his shoulder as the knot of tension within her began to disappear.

'And it frightens you,' he contributed, gently threading his fingers through her hair. 'I don't believe that seeing a bird hit a plate-glass window was the only reason you left New York. You must have had a pretty good reason for wanting to hide away in a quiet backwater like this.'

'To hide?' He'd struck more of a nerve than he knew, and she took refuge in resentment, trying to pull away, but finding herself held fast against him. 'Don't you mean that it's a fine place to maintain my virgin status?'

'That too, I suppose,' he agreed comfortably, ignoring her injured tone, 'but I don't think that's the real issue. You're as bad as I am, you know, except with you it's not pre-stressed concrete and developing nations. With you, it's virginity and an eccentric, post-hippie life-style.'

'I'm doing what I want to do.'

'Yes, and what you want most of all is to avoid something too painful to bear.'

'That's rubbish!'

'It's not, and you know it.' Without warning, he turned and carried her back into the cushions, the hard line of his body just above her, holding her captive. 'What's your secret, Marigold?'

'There isn't one,' she protested, tensing when she saw him bend his head towards her.

'Relax, love.' His lips touched her temple, then her cheek. 'This is just like ballooning.'

'It's not . . . Damn you, O'Neil,' she complained weakly, fighting a losing battle against the sudden wild beat of her heart and the languor invading her limbs. 'You think you can win every round.'

'We both win,' he corrected absently, his voice thickening now, his lips already teasing at hers, 'and it feels so good . . .'

Was that the word for it? she wondered vaguely as his lips took possession of hers with a clever deliberation which threatened to drive her mad. What he was doing to her was a kind of torment; he was teasing and withdrawing, returning to explore . . . destroying her defences. An impossible tension was building within her, leaving her with no choice but to let him guide her inexorably towards that final, endless moment of explosive need . . .

'Do you see what I mean?' he asked, his breathing nearly as erratic as her own. 'Now do you understand?'

'Understand?' she repeated, shaken to her very core, staring up at him with dazed, uncomprehending eyes. 'I can't even think . . .'

'Exactly, love. Sometimes it's better not to, and this was one of them.' His lips met hers again, differently this time—a gentle, undemanding kiss. 'But still . . . the time will come when you'll tell me what hurts so much. And when you trust me enough to do that, there won't be anything else to be afraid of.'

Then, before she could speak, or even gather her scattered thoughts, he rose in one lithe movement and was gone.

Mari knew it was time to tell O'Neil to keep his promise to leave. Nothing good could come of spending more time with him; he would only further upset the delicate balance she'd made of her life. He had ruffled her pond—damn him!—with the physical attraction which could so instantly flare between them.

Between them—that was the key. Never before had she felt something between herself and a man. When she had lived in New York, she had been casually involved with a few men, but none of them had possessed the depth or appeal or *whatever* to kindle the intense attraction she felt for O'Neil. Until O'Neil, she had never been kissed by a man—never kissed one in return—in a way to make her forget everything except desire and raw, aching need.

Never, until O'Neil . . . She had neither expected nor wanted anything like what O'Neil was doing to her. Serenity, peace and the freedom to do as she pleased were all she'd intended to ask of life—until O'Neil had appeared and blown even those modest hopes out of the water. But the worst of it was that he had now raised the stakes even higher—much too high. Physical attraction she could have handled; she might even have decided to have an affair with him, but she hadn't expected him to see that she was hiding something from the world, and she *certainly* hadn't expected him to link physical attraction to the demand that she tell him what she was hiding! O'Neil had a weapon no one else possessed, and if he was going to use it—use the damnable physical attraction that existed between them—to badger her into *telling* him . . . Well, there was no peace and serenity there!

She should tell him to leave. She *would* tell him to leave, she resolved; the only problem was that you couldn't tell a man to leave when he didn't come near you! For the better part of a week, she saw nothing of him. She knew he was there in his impersonal house at the top of the ridge; the helicopter had made no sudden departure. He was there, all right—playing games with her head, leaving her alone until she missed him . . . Well, it had been more than the few days he'd suggested; it had been nearly a week, and—damn it—she *was* missing him! And that was the best reason of all for telling him to leave, she realised, fired with the determination to end this business with O'Neil at the first opportunity.

But when she finally did see him again, when he entered her house without knocking and came upon her unannounced in her kitchen, his appearance took her breath away and scattered her thoughts. She could only stare blankly at him, up to her elbows in melon balls, her mouth undoubtedly hanging open.

'It looks as if you're planning an orgy,' he observed, taking in the array of fruit and freshly picked mint which covered every available surface in the small kitchen. 'Or have you taken it into your head to go into the catering business?'

'I'm making fruit salad.'

'For the whole town?'

'For a family picnic. We're a big family.' And she was running late, she reminded herself, using that thought for protection. She *knew* she should have started last night, so she returned to the task of scooping melon balls out of a honeydew, pausing only long enough to tell herself that this was the man who had been playing games with her head. 'I always get stuck with the watermelon basket on the Fourth of July.'

'Ah. I'd forgotten it was the Fourth.'

'That's because you don't spend enough time here. You're too busy in Third World countries with Independence Days of their own. Or else you hole up in your house and forget the rest of the world.'

'Is that a little gentle criticism, Mari?'

'No,' she told him, hoping that wasn't a lie. 'Merely an observation.'

'Or a complaint?' he persisted hopefully, then smiled when he saw her grim expression.

'Don't flatter yourself,' she snapped, hardening her heart against his appeal. 'I haven't got time for your games. I've got to get this damn thing done fast, or I won't be ready when Lily and Nate pick me up.'

'Can I help?'

'I don't know . . .' Damn! She was weakening, and she couldn't help herself. 'Can you make melon balls?'

'I can learn, and I haven't got anything else to do.'

'All right,' she conceded ungraciously, showing him what to do. When she was convinced he could manage, she set to work on the delicate task of sectioning out the top of the watermelon, working with her best butcher knife to form scalloped edges for the container to hold the rest of the fruit.

'So that's a watermelon basket,' he observed when she was done. 'I wouldn't have believed it.'

'Why? Haven't you ever seen one before?'

'Afraid not,' he answered cheerfully enough. 'My life hasn't run to things like family picnics and watermelon baskets. What do we do now? Dump all this other stuff in it?'

'After I line it with mint leaves,' she explained, starting the job, then pausing to glance frantically at the clock when she heard the sound of a car. 'Damn! They're here, and I'm nowhere near done, and Nate hates to be kept waiting . . .'

'Would it help if I ran you over when you are?' O'Neil offered with careful diffidence. 'I can't see you managing this on your bike.'

'If you don't mind,' she accepted grudgingly. Then, thinking about a life that hadn't run to family picnics, she impulsively offered, 'Do you want to come too?'

'Why not?' he responded calmly enough, but, behind his easy manner, Mari thought he seemed surprised. 'It ought to be fun.'

Perhaps O'Neil was having the fun he'd expected, Mari fumed, but *she* should have known better, should have known that including him in a family picnic would be a disaster. He was only one among twelve adults and seventeen children, but he had immediately become the centre of attention—an object of curiosity to the children and something far more important to the adults.

Her mother persisted in referring to him as 'Mari's young man', while her father's approach was to seize every possible opportunity to clap him on the back and call him 'my boy'. They obviously took it for granted that O'Neil had decided to marry their youngest daughter, while their son and three other daughters didn't seem so sure. Apparently they felt he needed more convincing, so they spent the day extolling Mari's virtues—selling her, she thought bitterly. They were doing their damnedest to insure that she achieved a safe and secure future as O'Neil's wife.

Today was a mistake, she brooded darkly, sitting alone and forgotten in the shade of an old maple tree. As Lily took her turn at persuasion, Mari told herself that she'd been a fool to bring O'Neil here. She had spent her whole life loving the members of her family in spite of their determination to smother her with well-meaning concern; she should have *known* that exposing them to O'Neil would only make things worse.

'Lord! They're quite a bunch,' O'Neil observed when he'd managed to extricate himself from the others to join Mari in the shade. 'They certainly care about you.'

'Too much,' Mari snapped, by this time coiled tight as a spring. 'When they haven't been selling you on my good points, have they been trying to find out of your intentions are honourable?'

'In one way or another, but I think I've sidestepped the issue quite well.' He leaned back on the grass, grinning up at her. 'I've been giving the impression that *my* intentions are strictly honourable, but that I'm not quite sure of *yours*.'

'You haven't!' she exclaimed, dissolving into helpless laughter. 'Oh, I wish I'd thought of that,' she managed at last. 'Thank you, O'Neil.'

'It seemed the least I could do.' He smiled up at her, wise and knowing. 'It's a good thing we're two of a kind, Marigold—both determined to remain unattached. Although——'

'Hey, you two!' called Violet, bearing down upon their shady spot. 'Not fair being anti-social on the Fourth of July, although even I wouldn't mind a quiet minute or two.' Gracefully, in spite of her advanced pregnancy, she lowered herself on to the grass, facing

Mari and O'Neil. 'Today, Junior here—and after four girls, this had better be Junior—feels like twins. Twins run in the family, you know,' she confided to O'Neil, 'although Lily's already had a set, so I hope I'm going to miss them. We all breed like rabbits,' she continued cheerfully. 'We're determined to equal or pass Mummy's record—except Mari, of course. Her biological clock is just ticking away, and she'll never make it if she doesn't get started soon.'

'Violet, *please*,' said through gritted teeth.

'Of course,' Violet continued, undeterred, fixing O'Neil with her clear-eyed gaze, 'you may not even care about Mari's biological clock.'

'I really hadn't given it much thought,' drawled O'Neil, his eyes alight with laughter, sharing it with Mari. 'She has so many other—more interesting —attributes.'

'That's certainly true,' Violet agreed approvingly. 'Besides, at your age, I don't suppose you'd want to be saddled with too many kids—and five is definitely too many, at least on occasion . . . and this is one of them,' she added, lumbering to her feet, calling out to one of her girls who was trying to force Jack's baby to eat a potato chip. 'Linsey, stop! He's not old enough to eat that! Time to play mother again,' she explained to O'Neil, making a rueful face at him, 'which is probably just as well. I've either put my foot badly in it, or done a marvellously effective job at playing matchmaker. Whatever I've done, Mari wants me to stop, so I'll leave you two lovebirds to sort it out.'

'Lovebirds,' Mari muttered under her breath. 'I could *kill* her! I could kill them all. Do you have any idea what it's like to be a twenty-nine-year-old and still have your parents and brother and sisters treating you like a baby?'

'None at all,' O'Neil acknowledged cheerfully, his gaze following the ebb and flow of activity, the unrehearsed choreography of parents and children on the lawn. 'I'm an only child, the product of singularly uninterested parents. This is all new to me, and—in spite of the matchmaking—a pleasure to watch and be a part of. They all seem so happy, as though family really matters to them.'

Which it did, Mari reflected, watching Violet bend down, her head close to Linsey's, presumably explaining why you couldn't feed potato chips to an infant. Jack's wife joined them, scooping up the baby to cradle him in her arms, and Mari found her attention captured by that unthinkingly protective gesture. Mothers and children, she thought wistfully, happy families that matter . . . a door forever closed to her. Unexpectedly, she was caught by the *unfairness* of it all, of what the others had that she never could, of what she had spent five years denying she wanted . . .

'And we've lost something, haven't we?' O'Neil asked quietly, and when Mari turned to look at him she saw the understanding in his eyes. 'There's a down side to staying unattached, but we're stuck with it—like it or not.'

'Yes,' Mari agreed tonelessly, suddenly not liking it at all.

CHAPTER FOUR

PERHAPS O'Neil's awareness of her doubts that day had made him uncomfortable, or perhaps her family's reaction to him had put him off. Whatever the reason, he managed—without saying a word or making an obvious change in their routine—to maintain a careful distance between them. For the rest of the summer, Mari found that she had no grounds for complaint that he was crowding her or making her care too much. Instead, their pattern of being together was almost too undemandingly safe.

His comings and goings were the key; he used or withheld his presence in a way that ensured that no intense intimacy could develop between them. Mari assumed that his trips were dictated by the demands of his work, but even in that he were the extra length to maintain his detachment, never telling her of his plans in advance. She would only know when he had left or come back when she heard the helicopter's swift passage over her house.

When he was in residence, they usually went up in his balloon once or twice a week, and in sharing their enthusiasm for the flight they were closer than at any other time. Other times, even when he came to share a meal with her, there was something about him—not really a stiffness, but a reserve . . . Often now, their time together was spent in what Mari had to characterise as formal dates. Arranged a few hours in advance, O'Neil would take her over into Stowe, driving a lethal-looking black Porsche, for dinner at an elegant restaurant, then dancing in a night-sport there. Careful times they were, Mari noted, times when their being together was tempered by the presence of strangers.

Their relationship was—in a word—detached, without any substance at all, Mari reflected more than once as the summer began to draw to a close. They still talked a great deal, about his work and hers, mutual interests, shared tastes. They still engaged in a certain amount of verbal sparring; it wasn't as though O'Neil had stopped reminding her that they would make love some time, but he didn't seem to feel the need to *do* anything about it. Except for the casual arm around her shoulders and the occasional even more casual kiss, he tried nothing at all.

And count yourself lucky for that! she lectured herself more than once when an evening with him was over and she was left feeling curiously incomplete. Your problem is that you don't know *what* you want! You know you don't want him to make love to you, but you'd like him at least to give it a *try!* But why? So you can have the satisfaction of turning him down? Because your ego could do with the boost of knowing he's still interested? Or is it because, even though you know you can't have the whole loaf, you'd like at least a part?

That, she concluded, was probably closest to the truth. O'Neil was, after all, an attractive man. No, 'attractive' wasn't the word she was after; O'Neil was an incredibly sexy man, whose kisses were dynamite, and whose touch . . . 'Damn! I've got it bad,' she told Founder. 'One brief and less than conclusive seduction scene in a meadow, and I'm practically lusting after the man! It's disgusting!' Then she sighed, her discontent magnified by the weather which had suddenly turned turned hellishly hot, a heavy, punishing heat that sapped both her strength and Founder's. By noon it was nearly a hundred degrees in the sun and not much better inside the house—too hot even to try to work, she decided, pushing aside her embroidery frame, going outside in search of a breeze.

There wasn't one, of course—that would have been asking too much, she thought crossly. There did, however, seem to be a slightly lesser stillness of air on the rise behind the house. There, one of the maple trees grew so close to the second growth on the ridge that their branches mingled, creating deep shade. Mari spread the sheet she had brought out with her and lay down upon it, her arms crossed behind her head. 'If I don't move, I'll be cool,' she said to the tangle of branches above her, applying the power of positive thinking as she closed her eyes.

She wanted to sleep; instead, she found herself thinking about O'Neil, wondering if he would come to visit today. It was maddening never to know what to expect of him! He kept her perpetually off balance, and she was certain of nothing about him—except that he always withheld more than he gave, while she increasingly wanted more . . .

'Mari? Are you sleeping?'

She came awake slowly, staring up into O'Neil's tanned, clever face. 'I must have been,' she allowed, on the edge of a yawn. 'It's so hot.'

'True,' he agreed cheerfully, lowering himself on to the other side of the sheet, 'but not as hot as where I'll be tomorrow.'

'So—you're leaving again?' He looked, she thought, as thought he'd already left, was already in some obscure and even more hellishly hot part of the world. He was wearing khaki shorts and a matching cotton bush shirt, the shirt unbuttoned enough to reveal a fair bit of teak-dark, impressively muscled flesh, his sunglasses with their aviator frames hiding his eyes. 'Heavens,' she murmured, closing her eyes against the impact of him, 'that doesn't bear thinking about.'

'Ah. Does that mean you're going to miss me?'

'Of course not.' The answer was automatic, unthinking, her mind busy with something else. 'Missing you isn't part of the game.' But today he was playing a different game, or had raised the stakes in the game they were playing . . . but *why*? 'You've never done this before—at least not since . . . not for a long time. Given me any warning that you were leaving, I mean.'

'That's right,' he agreed unhelpfully.

'So why do it today?' Mari pushed herself up into a sitting position, staring down at him, wishing he'd take his sunglasses off. 'Are you trying to get an edge, O'Neil? Am I supposed to feel so bad that you're leaving that you can seduce me and then leave in the morning?'

'No. I'm still prepared to wait until you decide to seduce me.'

'And in the meantime, whenever your frustration level gets too high, you can go jetting off to some Third World country and have your way with Third World women.'

'Is that what you think?' Now he did take off his glasses, and she almost wished he hadn't. His eyes were half closed, but his lashes—absurdly long for a man, she thought, wondering why she had never noticed them before—couldn't completely conceal the lazy spark of amusement lurking in those deep blue depths. 'Love, you're wrong,' he murmured, capturing her hand, bringing it to his lips to scatter small kisses across her fingers. 'I'm not some green youth with a frustration level that gets unbearably high. I've gone far beyond that point.' He turned her hand, briefly kissing the pulse that beat at her wrist. 'I don't want any substitutes.' Now he laced his fingers through hers to open her hand, and she felt his lips feather against her palm when he spoke again. 'I'm waiting for you.'

'Don't!' she implored, even as her fingers moved of their own volition to rest against his cheek and the hard, clean line of his jaw. 'O'Neil, don't tease me!'

'I'm not teasing you. This is real.' He moved her hand to his chest, pressing it against his flesh, so that she could feel the racing beat of his heart. 'Can't you tell?' he asked with a slow, utterly unselfconscious smile.

'No . . . yes . . .' Damn! She was so confused, her heart already racing as fast as his. She was bending over him now, and even when he released her hand it stayed motionless against the beat of his heart. 'I don't know.'

'Yes, you do.' He reached up with both hands, threading his fingers through her hair until it fell, a wild tangle of curls, around her face. 'Lord, you're a beautiful girl,' he told her, an abstracted smile playing at the corners of his mouth. 'Kiss me, love.'

'I shouldn't,' she whispered, but she had no choice. The lazy spark of desire in his half-closed eyes had already kindled an answering need in her; her pulse wasn't just racing now, it was pounding—matching the beat of his heart beneath her hand. Desire—his and her own—had bound them together and now drew her lips, already parted, to his.

'That's right . . . sweet Mari,' he breathed between small, fiery kisses. 'Lord . . . what you're doing to me!' he managed before his mouth captured hers.

He took possession of her with the intimacy of his probing invasion, compelling her to return his kiss with a wild and unthinking abandon. She felt giddy, light-headed and totally free to savour the extraordinary sharing between them, the exultant fusion of his lips to hers, and his touch—like fire as he caressed the high curve of her breast.

At last! she thought when he lifted her on to the taut line of his body, moulding her hips to his own. She felt his legs tangling with hers, then he turned with her and the hard weight of his body closed over hers. This was what she'd been wanting from him all along, she recognised vaguely. He was making real what she had never before understood, never realised she wanted . . . All those empty years before O'Neil, she mused dreamily, gripping his shoulders, holding him to her as a fierce wave of desire broke over her.

'Mari . . . love . . .' He drew a shuddering breath when their kiss finally ended. 'Are we going too fast?'

Dazed, she shook her head, reaching up to brush the thick slant of hair back from his forehead. 'No. Not with you, and not when it feels so right.'

'Are you sure?'

'I don't want to talk about sure,' she complained, linking her arms around his neck to draw his lips back to the aching need of hers. 'I don't want to think any more. I just want you to make it happen, O'Neil.'

'In other words, the responsibility's mine,' he said flatly, and she could feel his withdrawal, see the spark of desire in his eyes fading away, being replaced by cool and objective detachment. 'You want me to decide.'

'What's wrong with that?' she coaxed, smoothing her hands down his back while she stirred beneath him, instinctively doing whatever she could to rekindle the flame. 'It's what I want—I know that now—and it's happening. Please don't let it stop.'

'Sorry, love, but that's not what I want.' In one quick movement he turned, and they were suddenly lying side by side on the sheet, a small distance between them. 'Don't you see?' he continued more kindly. 'You had no intention of letting this happen this afternoon. It wouldn't have happened if I hadn't started things and then let them go on too long.'

'Then what am I supposed to do?' she asked unhappily. 'I can't just start this kind of thing by myself. I don't know *how*! That's why this seemed like the right time, because *you* started it and—this is embarrassing!—and all *I* had to do was let it keep going.'

'But it's not the right way,' he insisted stubbornly. 'You know I want you, have been wanting you all this long summer. It's been so hard, love, keeping my distance, waiting to see how you felt, what you wanted. And today . . . Perhaps it was knowing I had to leave, that I wouldn't be seeing you for *too* long. Damn! I was wanting—needing—something, but it wasn't the right thing to do. Mari, love, I was *taking*, and how can I take what you haven't been willing to *give* anyone for twenty-nine years?'

'Do you have to be so damn noble?' She managed a smile. 'It's just my luck to meet a man who cares enough about me to not want to force the issue. O'Neil, for someone who says he doesn't want to care, you're caring almost *too* much about me! I wish——' she wavered briefly, then cast caution to the winds, moved a little closer and slipped her arms around him '—I wish you wouldn't be quite such a gentleman about this.'

'I won't be, if you keep this up,' he warned as she moved even closer, finally erasing the last of the distance between them.

'I must be learning,' she teased, twisting slightly so that her breasts could brush lightly against his chest, the thin muslin of her dress no real barrier between them. '*Am* I learning, O'Neil?' she whispered, smiling when she felt him draw a quick, sharp breath.

'Damn right you are,' he answered unsteadily, 'and don't ever tell me again that you don't know what to do.'

'It's easier than I thought,' she confided, pressing her lips to the firm edge of his jaw, 'and it's fun . . .' Her lips moved down, tasting the fine filming of salt on the strong column of his throat, listening to his harsh and unsteady breathing—and suddenly it wasn't fun any more. It was *real*—incredibly real and important—this awesome and irrevocable step she was trying to take. 'If I only didn't have to think,' she whispered, suddenly weary, resting her head on his shoulder. 'If I could just forget everything . . . not worry about what this will mean.'

'I know.'

'No, you don't.' As quickly as it had come, the wanting—the longing—was gone. 'I'm afraid,' she confessed unsteadily. 'I'm still afraid that you'll matter too much. Perhaps you already do. You're right, O'Neil—I'm not ready yet.' Reluctantly she pulled away, re-establishing the careful distance between them. 'It's a good thing you're going away, because I've got to think, got to decide what I want, or what I can handle. As my father is fond of saying, it's time to fish or cut bait.'

'Dear heaven, Mari,' he said on an unsteady note of laughter, 'only you could put it quite that way!'

'Well, it's true,' she insisted with a tentative smile. 'It's not fair to you, to keep playing this game, and I'm beginning to think that it's not fair to me. At least, it's not easy or terribly pleasant. It's . . .'

'Frustrating?' he suggested drily, and then they both laughed.

'Yes! I never *knew* . . .' She watched, absorbing the play of muscles beneath smooth brown skin as he got to his feet and extended his hand to her. 'I'll sort this all out while you're gone,' she promised, standing before him, still holding his hand. 'I *will* have a decision for you when you get back.'

For an instant his eyes were pained, even haunted, before he smiled the off-centre grin she now knew so well. 'I can't ask for more than that, can I?' Then he gathered her into his arms, kissing her with an odd combination of gentleness and insistence which left her feeling close to tears. 'I'll—I'll think of you,' he finished, turning away to disappear into the leafy shade of the path to the top of the ridge.

For nearly two weeks Mari was mostly alone in her little house, with only Founder for companionship. Like an automaton, she structured her days, filling the hours with large and small tasks to keep herself busy. But all the work in the world couldn't keep her from missing O'Neil, a fact which—once acknowledged— left her confused.

She hadn't expected to miss him; she'd expected to feel relief at having been given some breathing-room. After all, she had some serious thinking to do, a decision to make, and it could be better done without the distraction of his always magnetic, often over-whelming and occasionally irresistible presence. More to the point, missing O'Neil was incontrovertible

proof that it was already too late to protect herself
from the emotional entanglements she had neither
wanted nor needed. At some point during the
summer, without realising that it had happened, she
had crossed her own line between detachment and
involvement. Like it or not, O'Neil was part of her life
now—not just pretty stitches on the surface of the
cloth, but part of the close-woven fabric upon which
the design was worked. So, in her isolation, Mari
missed him—most of all in the evenings when her
day's work was done. As the night closed in, heavy
with the sound of crickets, she could finally allow her
thoughts—and her imagination—free rein.

She began a piece of work of a kind she had never
attempted before, a whimsical landscape brought to
life with shimmering silk thread. Each evening she
completed a little more of the design, until finally she
could begin to see what her mind had created. It was a
view which included O'Neil's house on the ridge, her
own tucked below, the ribbon of road and the covered
bridge, the rooftops and the white church spire in the
village, the mountains gently massed on either side of
the valley. Above it all, against the soft tints of
twilight, floated the kaleidoscope of colour that was
O'Neil's balloon.

The work, using her needle to bring colour and
texture and form, kept her fingers busy, while her
thoughts—like the balloon, she decided in an almost
literal flight of fancy—floated above the landscape of
her feelings and desires. She wanted O'Neil; it was as
simple as that. It was too late to worry about getting
involved, about protecting herself from the pain of
one more attachment to life. O'Neil was a part of her
now; sending him away wouldn't accomplish a thing.

Still, her decision was of such magnitude that it

frightened her, and the fear stayed with her until the moment when Founder grew restless and began to pace and whine. By now she didn't need to wonder why; she knew O'Neil was coming, that in a few minutes she would hear the first faint sounds of the helicopter.

Suddenly, in the space of those few minutes, all her fear disappeared. She had, she discovered with a curious lightening of her heart, nothing to lose. She trusted O'Neil, but more than that, she now had the courage within her to admit that she loved him. If things had been different for them, she suddenly realised, if she had more time—if she had forever—she would have wanted forever with him.

Well, you don't have forever, she told herself, already moving towards the door, but at least you have *now*! Use it, enjoy it! Don't be afraid! It was so incredibly simple, she realised, running outside as the sound of the helicopter grew louder. By the time she saw it, she was clear of the trees, waving madly, wondering if he could see her. 'I love you, O'Neil!' she shouted, her words drowned by the roar of the ungainly machine passing overhead. 'I love you, and the answer is yes—let's do it! I *want* to make love!'

He saw her; she knew he did, because the helicopter banked slightly and then turned, completing a wide circle over the house before heading off towards the ridge. 'Well, he knows,' she remarked to the sky, starting slowly back to the house. 'He may not have heard what I said, but he surely knows.'

When she reached the stepping-stone by the door, she sat down to wait in the last rays of the setting sun. There was autumn in the air; she noticed it for the first time, wrapping her arms around her for warmth. He had left on the hottest day of the summer and

come back on the first evening she might want a fire.
There was a certain symmetry there, she decided,
closing her eyes. Perhaps they had come as close to
full circle as they could . . .

'Mari.'

Heavens! She hadn't expected him quite so soon,
and she found herself suddenly shy. Perhaps *he* didn't
know the extent to which she'd declared herself—after
all, he couldn't have heard the words she had shouted
at the sky!—but she suddenly felt exposed, afraid that
he might see too clearly what she was feeling—afraid
that he might have changed his mind . . . She delayed
opening her eyes for a moment, and when she did she
only made things worse for herself.

It was hard to believe it was O'Neil who stood
before her; this man seemed like a stranger,
resplendent in a navy pin-stripe suit, crisp white shirt
and navy and maroon silk tie, his eyes hidden behind
the aviator-frame dark glasses which were the only
thing familiar to her. 'O'Neil?' she asked doubtfully,
and was rewarded with his unmistakable off-centre
grin. 'You're wearing a suit,' she accused.

'Because I came straight from the chopper. I saw
you wave.' Deliberately, he took off the dark glasses,
and she saw that his eyes were a deeper blue than ever
before, drawing colour from the deep blue of his suit.
Deeper blue and seeing things more clearly, she
thought, her own gaze skittering away from his to
follow the movements of his long, slender hands as
she folded the glasses and tucked them into a pocket.
'You've never waved before.'

'I know.' She hesitated, still watching his hands.
'Have I given myself away?'

'I hope so,' he said, with such feeling that it
banished her doubts and her shyness; and when he

held out his arms she went to him without hesitation. 'Mari . . . love,' he murmured unsteadily, holding her very close. 'It may be against the rules, but I've missed you.'

'I've missed you too,' she confessed, and when she wrapped her arms around his neck, he lifted her off her feet.

'Thank heavens!' he managed just before he kissed her, briefly, but with satisfying thoroughness. 'Lord, I've been thinking of this, dreaming about it, and hoping . . .' He kissed her again, gently this time, then set her on her feet so that they could go into the house. 'Is staying away too long what's made you so glad to see you?'

'No. Yes. Partly,' she told him, watching him bend to greet Founder. Now what? she wondered distractedly, terribly aware of his presence in the gathering shadows of her little room. A few minutes ago, she had decided what to do, but she hadn't considered the details of getting it done. Did she just baldly tell him she wanted to sleep with him now? Or was there some better, subtler way—some way she would know if she'd ever done this sort of thing before? 'O'Neil,' she plunged in, painfully aware that she was blushing, but determined to get past this point, 'I've made up my mind, but for all I know, you've changed yours . . . I mean, it seems a little nervy just to announce it flat out, but I'm not sure what else——You can't have any idea how hard this is,' she continued doggedly. 'I mean, you've had so much more experience——'

'Not as much as you seem to think.' He smiled, abandoning Founder to take both her hands in his. 'Mari, I may not have lived like a monk all these years, but I'm not exactly a hardened roué.'

'You're still light years ahead of me,' she snapped. 'Damn it, O'Neil, I don't know what I'm supposed to do next!'

'You could start by giving me supper,' he suggested hopefully. 'The last time I remember eating was last night on the plane.'

'Of course! I should have thought of that.' Hastily she extracted her hands from his grasp and made for the kitchen, grateful to be presented with a concrete task. 'I'm not sure what I have, though,' she explained doubtfully, surveying the meagre contents of the refrigerator. 'I was going to have salad and cheese, but the night's turning cool, and it's not much when you haven't eaten for so long. I could give you eggs and Canadian bacon.'

'That's what you gave me the first time,' he reminded her from his now accustomed place in the kitchen door. 'Why not do it again? There's a kind of symmetry there.'

'As though we'd come full circle,' she supplied, completing both his thought and the one she had been thinking while she waited for him to come. It was uncanny, something unexplainable—unless being in love could explain it—and she could only stand motionless, hugging her happiness to her until she remembered herself and set to work on their meal.

In silence, leaning against the doorframe, he watched her, his gaze following her quick, sure movements, not moving himself until she had assembled the things for the table. 'I'll do that,' he offered, taking the plates and cutlery from her, switching on a light as he went into the living-room.

Now it was her turn to watch him. She stood in the doorway, seeing him move with a casual grace that tore at her heart. He set the table, then shed his jacket and tie, carelessly tossing them on to a chair. Unaware that she was watching, he stood for a moment in the centre of the room, freeing the top few buttons of his shirt, then working with brief economy to remove his cuff-links. They made a small sound in the silence as he dropped them on the table before rolling up his shirtsleeves to reveal the contrast between his deep tan and the whiteness of his shirt. Finally he stripped off his watch, bending to place it beside the cuff-links, flexing his shoulders as he straightened up again. 'There. I hope you don't mind,' he offered when at last he saw her in the doorway, 'but I feel more human now.'

'You look more like yourself. I'm not used to you in a suit.'

'Neither am I,' he admitted, coming to stand in the doorway again, 'but I had to spend today in New York, on my way back to you. A suit is one of the few concessions I make to the city—which is why I spend as little time as possible there. I expect you can understand that.'

'Oh, yes.' She turned away from his lazy smile, hunting through the cutlery drawer for her corkscrew, then bringing forth the bottle of wine that had been sitting in the refrigerator for over a week. 'Can you do this?' she asked, handing both to him. 'I'm hopeless with corks.'

'What is it?' he asked, doubtfully regarding the unlabelled bottle.

'Peach wine, from one of my sewing ladies. Her son makes it, and she says it's very good.'

'*Peach* wine?' One eyebrow spoke volumes. 'Not dandelion or elderberry?'

'I know, I never heard of it either, but it's all I've got. The last time I served eggs and Canadian bacon to a man, *he* brought champagne. Dom Perignon,' she added reproachfully.

'Perhaps you should have stuck with him,' he advised, setting to work on the cork. '*I* come empty-handed and expect to be fed.'

'I know, but I like you better. *He* was a stranger.'

'Do you make a habit of entertaining strangers, letting them ply you with champagne?'

'No. I'd never done it before.' She turned away to concentrate on pouring the eggs into the pan, adding to herself, '. . . but I'm glad I did it that one time.'

'I heard that, Marigold Scott.' He came up behind her, slipping his arms around her waist to draw her back against him. 'This is grand,' he told her, his lips at her temple. 'It makes things between us entirely different. More . . .'

'Domestic?'

'Incredibly so,' he agreed on a deeper note, 'and I love it.'

'You won't love it so much if I burn the eggs.'

'True.' Instantly he released her. 'First things first, I suppose, and I really am hungry.'

'I can't believe you're eating this mess,' Mari told him a few minutes later, eating very little herself to watch him consume the lion's share of what was an admittedly bizarre combination—scrambled eggs, Canadian bacon, raisin bread with sweet butter, a lemon-tarragon dressed salad and the peach wine. 'You must have been starving.'

'Close to it,' he allowed between mouthfuls. 'It was too hot to want to eat, most of the time. Besides, I was pining for you. Do you mind that I say that?'

'Not tonight.' In fact, she liked the idea that he had been pining for her, although she supposed that she shouldn't. It must be the peach wine, she decided, belatedly realising that she'd had rather a lot of it on a nearly empty stomach. How else to explain why she wasn't bothered by the fact that things were moving very fast—perhaps too fast—between them? There was more to it, she thought, than her simple decision that they should make love. They were both saying things they hadn't said before, both making it clear that they *cared*. It wasn't wise, but tonight she didn't *want* to be wise! She wanted to be free and happy and close to O'Neil.

'You're thinking very hard about something,' he observed, penetrating her rosy, reckless glow. 'Having second thoughts?'

'None at all,' she answered, and meant it, even though it was obvious that the moment of truth was nearly upon her. While she had been thinking, he had finished eating—had finished everything there was to eat, in fact—amd was watching her now with an expectant, *waiting* expression. It was time to make love, she realised with a tiny shiver of anticipation, but with no sense of panic or nerves. She still didn't know how to handle the details, but that didn't matter. She trusted O'Neil, and he would manage things. 'I've been thinking about you and me. About *us*.'

'Good.' He stood up, offering his hand. 'And what have you decided?'

'You know!' She ignored his outstretched hand, standing on tiptoe to fling her arms around his neck. 'It's time for us, O'Neil. I don't want to wait any longer.'

'No?'

'No!' She waited for him to kiss her, and when he didn't do so immediately she pressed even closer to him, accommodating the curves of her body to the

lean, hard strength of his. I'm being absolutely
shameless, she realised, caressing the nape of his neck,
letting her fingers tangle in his crisp hair. I'm doing
my best to seduce him . . . which is what he wanted,
although I didn't think I'd know how . . . It must be
the wine . . . and O'Neil—a potent combination, those
two. 'O'Neil, why don't you kiss me?'

'Because—— Lord, Mari! You're almost too hard to
resist!'

'Then don't,' she urged, watching him bend his head,
her lips parting instantly to the pressure of his. Oh, yes!
she thought as their kiss deepened, as they tempted and
teased, each testing the other's hunger and need.
Without ending their kiss, O'Neil lifted her off her feet,
cradling her in his arms as he carried her to the couch
and sat down, holding her on his lap. 'Why here?' she
asked when he ended their kiss to draw a long,
shuddering breath. 'We can go up to my room.'

'No . . . we've got to talk.'

'I don't want to talk,' she complained, smoothing
her hands over the fine linen of his shirt, savouring
the hard muscles beneath. 'I want to make love.'

'I'm well aware of that,' he acknowledged drily, and
she tried to ignore the new note of self-possession in
his voice, 'but we need to talk. Mari, things have
changed.'

'Changed how?' she asked vaguely, pressing her lips
to the strong column of his throat.

'I've broken the rules—Mari! *Listen* to me,' he
commanded, shifting slightly, forcing just a little
space between them. 'Damn it! I've fallen in love with
you.'

'Oh, well . . . is that all?' She smiled, leaning
forward to rest her head on his chest. 'That's all right,
O'Neil, because I'm afraid I've fallen in love with you,

too.'

'Mari, I want——*What*? Do you mean that?' he demanded, as her words finally penetrated. 'Are you sure it's not just that you've had too much peach wine?'

'I know I've had too much peach wine,' she acknowledged dreamily, 'but that's not why I love you. I knew it before I'd had even a drop of peach wine. I knew it when you flew over the house. I told you so too. I yelled it as loud as I could, but you couldn't have heard me. So you see? So much for the rules! We've both broken the rules, but I don't mind if you don't. It's still all right. I mean, we don't have to worry, because we're not going to *do* anything about it—except make love, of course.' Lord, there's something wrong, she realised, seeing his grim expression. Perhaps the rules do matter to him, now that he knows that I've broken them too. It's all right for him to love me only if I don't love him back—is that it? Damn! I'm so muddled, and I've got to think how to reassure him, try to remember the arguments I used on myself, but that peach wine's done a number on me. If Lillian Downey ever offers me another bottle, I swear I won't take it!

But it's not just the peach wine, she acknowledged, continuing her dialogue with herself. It's wanting to make love with O'Neil—that's muddled me at least as much as the peach wine. I've been wanting to make love with him for so long. For forever, it seems. And we'll do it, just as soon as I can get these tedious explanations out of the way, get that grim expression off his face. Once he understands how I feel . . .

'O'Neil, it's all right—all right to feel the way we both do,' she began again, trying to marshal her scattered thoughts. 'You don't need to worry, because there still aren't any strings attached. Just because I love you too, there aren't any complications for you. I know you don't want to get married, and I don't expect you to marry me. I don't *want* you to marry me! So everything's *fine,*' she finished expansively, smiling up at him, her smile wavering uncertainly and then fading when she saw his expression, as grim as before. 'What's wrong?'

'Damn near everything! Mari, you're wrong about me. When I told you I'd broken the rules, I meant *all* of them. Mari . . . love——' He stopped to draw a deep breath. 'I *do* want us to get married! I can't think of anything I want more than to marry you.'

'No! You can't mean that!' Instantly she was cold sober, cold inside, just a hair's breadth away from panic. 'After everything you said—all your promises—how can you change your mind now?'

'Because *I've* changed, love. Because I was a fool to think I could let myself get so deeply involved and *not* change. Because I've learned that no matter how afraid I've been of involvement, of what can happen, of being hurt, I'm even more afraid of what life will be like without you. Mari love, you mean so much. Will you marry me?'

'*No!*' She closed her eyes, refusing to look at him, unable to face the love and appeal in his eyes. 'Damn you, O'Neil! How could you *do* this to me?'

'Because I believed—hoped, I suppose—that you were changing too—that whatever it was that made you feel so strongly about not getting involved was going away.'

'Well, it *hasn't*! Nothing about me has changed, and nothing about how I feel will *ever* go away!'

'But if you love me——'

'That doesn't change how I feel about getting

involved—about getting married!' Instinctively she straightened up, pushing against his chest, trying to free herself. 'Nothing's ever going to change that—not as long as I live!'

'But why, love?' he asked, the gentle question an odd contrast to his actions, his arms tightening around her, holding her fast when she tried to get up. 'What's hurt you so much that you still feel that way?'

'Nothing,' she answered fiercely, her back still rigid, her hands still spread against her chest, trying to resist both his superior physical strength and the compassion—the caring—in his voice. Don't give in now! she urged herself, fighting the panicky fear which was rising withing her. If he would be angry, she could fight him, but this kindness threatened to be her undoing. She couldn't bear kindness; it weakened her resolve, left her vulnerable, afraid of what she might give away. 'Damn you, O'Neil! If loving you is what's done this—made you feel this way—then I *won't!* I'll *stop* loving you! I already have!'

'No. That's not true, love. It's already too late . . .' He studied her face, his eyes dark and brooding, pleading with her. 'Mari love, I've been honest with you tonight. Can't you at least be as honest with me?'

CHAPTER FIVE

'DON'T do this to me!' Mari pushed against him with all her strength, and either because she had caught him by surprise or because he had made the decision to permit her to go, she wrenched herself free. Instantly she was on her feet and across the room.

She found herself at the table, gripping the edge, holding on for dear life, staring down at the casual disorder left from their meal. Oh, she'd been so happy during that meal; so happy when she'd been getting it ready; so happy when he'd come, when she'd been thinking about how the evening would end—and now *this*! It had all blown up in her face—when he'd asked the impossible of her. 'Marry me. Be honest with me.' She was trapped, left with no choice but to destroy both his happiness and her own.

'I can't tell you,' she said, willing her voice to be firm. 'I *won't*!'

'Mari, please. Whatever it is, it can't be that bad!'

Worse than that, she thought, still staring fixedly at the table. It's worse than bad. It's never . . . forever . . . nothing. The end. She couldn't breathe, she discovered. There was a pain inside her like nothing she'd ever felt before, a raw and burning ache she couldn't bear. She would never see O'Neil again, and the rest of her life—however long or short it would prove to be—didn't matter . . .

'*Tell* me, love!' In the silence, she heard him get up from the couch, heard his footsteps coming towards her. 'Whatever it is, we'll handle it, deal with it together.'

'Not this! We can't, O'Neil.' Until she spoke, she hadn't known she was crying, and now, before she could lift her hand to try to wipe away the tears, she felt herself being turned and folded into his embrace.

'Mari, love, don't be alone with this.' He held her close, one hand against her hair. 'Whatever it is, no matter how bad, don't be alone with it any longer. Tell me what it is.'

How she wanted to! After all these years of silence, she didn't want to be alone with it, and she felt so well-protected in his arms. But the habits of the last five years, the grim—fanatical—determination still held her in its grip. 'We never should have met,' she said now, through her tears. 'I never should have let this happen, let things go so far. I should have known, and now I've been so unfair to you . . . to both of us.'

'How, Mari?' His voice was just above her, calm and steady, infinitely patient—and compelling. 'How have you been unfair to us?'

'Because.' She was caught in a strange, dream-like confusion, half the terror of her trap and half the safety of O'Neil's presence—rock-solid, holding her, his strength enough to handle anything, while she had none. She had fought too long, too hard; whatever strength she'd had was gone, and now she had no choice. 'I'm going to die.'

'Tell me more, love.'

He had understood what she had said—she *knew* he had—but there had been no raw reaction in his voice, no involuntary contraction of his muscles as he held her. She'd told him the unthinkable and his strength was still intact, and that was what finally shattered her years of silence. 'Nearly five years ago, the doctor told me,' she began raggedly, still crying—crying harder now, the words coming unevenly, in tattered fragments. 'He said I only had about five years—which means the time is nearly up. I can't be sure exactly when—it's not as though they can tell you these things, but I suppose it could be any time. And I shouldn't have done this to you!'

'Never mind that now. What doctor told you this?'

'One in New York.' What difference did that make?

'Could he be *sure*? Did he know what he was saying?'

'Oh, yes, he was a specialist. I went to my own doctor first—because I was having headaches—and he sent me to the specialist. There were all kinds of tests, and then he told me.'

'And since then, has there been any change?'

'I don't think so.' His strength was pulling her together, his precise and unemotional questioning forcing her to give him the answers. 'I haven't had the headaches since I left New York, but they weren't part of the problem anyway. They were only stress—because I'd been working too hard.'

'Then what's the problem?'

'Something I was born with—a blood vessel in my brain that wasn't formed right. They can't do anything to fix it, and sooner or later it's just going to go, and because of where mine is—a lot of them are in the same general area—I won't make it. The doctor said he'd never known anyone with what I've got to live past thirty, and I'm twenty-nine.'

'And nothing has changed? Since he made the diagnosis, he hasn't been able to tell you anything new?'

'I don't know. I haven't seen him again.'

'Then we'll start there. Tomorrow we'll go to New York and see him again.'

'But there's no point,' she objected dully, feeling drained, suddenly so tired that even in O'Neil's arms she wasn't sure how much longer she could stay on her feet. 'He's a specialist, a good man in his field, and something like what I've got can't change.'

'But techniques change, treatments change, and five years is a long time in medicine.'

He sounded so sure, but so had the doctor. 'I don't know,' she said with a sigh.

'Of course you don't—not now. You've had too much for one day.' For the second time he picked her up, cradling her in his arms as he started up the stairs. 'You're going to bed now.'

Wearily she leaned her head against his shoulder, vaguely aware of how remarkable it was that she should be letting him take charge like this. She couldn't remember when she had ever willingly let anyone take charge of her—*for* her—before. Not since she'd been too young to resent her family's smothering attention, she supposed, but this was somehow different. O'Neil was holding her together; she was using him. But only for a little while, she promised herself. She couldn't let this present mood—this tired, empty, passive one—continue. She would have to get back her self-reliance and control, but just now she lacked the energy to do it. And all because O'Neil had stormed her defences and forced her to tell him what she had never told anyone else, she mused.

'Pyjamas? Nightgown?' she heard him ask as he set her set her down on the edge of the bed. 'Where should I look?'

'The top drawer.' She gestured briefly towards her chest of drawers, waiting passively until he returned with a clean nightgown.

'Put this on,' he told her. 'I'll be back in a minute.'

She forced herself to do as he said, stripping off her clothes, dropping them on the floor before pulling on

the nightgown. Then she sat down on the edge of the
bed again, closing her eyes while she waited for O'Neil

This all felt very much like a dream, she realised
Perhaps it *was* a dream; perhaps O'Neil hadn't come
back after all, perhaps she was dreaming this whole
evening. Was it a dream? she wondered, aware of his
presence beside her, turning obediently towards him so
that he could wash her tear-stained face. It could well be
a dream; in fact it must be a dream. It was so precisely
what she wanted and needed now—to be cared for, cared
about . . .

'Now bed,' he instructed, helping her in, pulling the
covers over her. Then, as though reading her half-
formed thoughts and knowing that she didn't want to be
left alone, he went around to the other side of the bed,
took off his shoes and emptied his pockets. 'Go to sleep,
love,' he told her, lying down beside her, drawing her
close, his arms securely around her. 'Don't think any
more. Just sleep.'

Mari nodded, still obedient, then released a long sigh.
'I'm sorry I did this to you,' she remembered to say. 'I
tried to keep it from happening. But thank you for being
so good.' She heard him say something in response, but
she was too tired to make out the words, too tired to
keep her eyes open, too tired even to try . . .

She came slowly awake, first aware of birds singing, of
O'Neil's long form beside her, of his arms still around
her. When she opened her eyes, the room was flooded
with light and O'Neil's gaze was fastened on her face.

'Good morning, love,' he said with a slow smile. 'How
do you feel?'

'I'm fine.' She had answered automatically, but she
did in fact feel fine, still pleasantly sleepy, and warm and
safe in his arms. She certainly felt better than he

looked, she saw now that she was a little more awake. There were dark circles under his eyes, and the lines in his face were more deeply etched than they had been the night before. 'Did you sleep at all?'

'Off and on.' This time his smile was slightly self-conscious. 'Contrary to what you seem to think, I'm not all that accustomed to having a woman in bed with me.'

But there was more to why he hadn't slept than that, she thought with a pang, remembering how she'd unburdened herself to him. Unfair, Mari! You've been so unfair to him. 'I've never seen you before when you needed to shave,' she remarked, experimentally running the palm of her hand over the shadow on the sharp line of his jaw, then smoothing back the thick slant of hair from his forehead. 'Poor O'Neil,' she whispered, her hand on his cheek as she leaned closer, kissing him briefly. 'You were so good to me last night, but I asked too much of you.'

'No, love.' He turned his head to touch her palm with his lips. 'You didn't ask—remember? I forced the issue, and I'm sorry for that.'

'No, you shouldn't be. I feel better for finally being honest with you—or I would if I hadn't burdened you with so much.'

'It's no burden.' He gathered her a little closer. 'Nor are you, darling Mari, not when you wake up in my arms.'

'Mmm.' She stretched luxuriously, then kissed him again. 'I wouldn't mind doing this every morning for the rest——' She stopped abruptly, the reality—and the pain—hard upon her again. 'Damn,' she whispered, wondering how, after all the crying she had done the night before, tears could possibly threaten again. 'I shouldn't have said that.'

'It doesn't matter,' he told her, 'because today we're

going to start doing something about that. You're going to be stuck with the rest of your life—and with me, like it or not. You'll see.'

She nodded, not trusting her voice. He made it all sound so simple when it wasn't, she thought, aching inside. He thought there could be a happy ending, but she knew better.

'I'll go up to my place to shower and change, and make sure the chopper is ready to go,' he told her. 'Will you be all right?'

'Of course,' she replied, forcing a bright note into her voice, forcing a smile. 'I'm not fragile, O'Neil.'

'If you say so.' He was suddenly more like himself, a sceptical gleam in his eyes as he studied her face, then kissed her soundly. 'Get dressed while I'm gone, love,' he instructed, releasing her and getting up, 'and pack a few things to take with you. This may take a few days.'

But it wouldn't, she told herself when he was gone. It would take only an hour or two for the doctor to tell O'Neil what she had heard five years before. He could hope now, but she knew better; there was no point to this trip to New York. Still, she got up, showered and dressed, then carefully packed her small suitcase.

How long would it be like this? she wondered, going downstairs to let Founder out and make herself a cup of instant coffee, perching on one of the tall stools at the counter. Nothing was the same between them now; all the fun of being together was gone. Because of what she'd told him, he hadn't been able to sleep last night; he'd felt the need to ask if she would be all right while he left her for just a short time. He would hover now, constantly worried about her, afraid that something would happen—that she would break, or perhaps even die in a moment when he wasn't there. And, for her, everything had become pretence. She was going along with this useless trip to New York just to please him; she was already weighing every word she said, trying to reassure or at least not worry him.

As she had feared from the start, it had become too complicated—and all because of her momentary weakness last night. And because they cared, she acknowledged, finding no comfort in that. It would have been simpler if they didn't care, if they had merely had a casual affair based on nothing but physical need, and then parted. She had been playing with fire these last few months; now both of them were being burned, and the pain would continue until——Until when? she asked herself, resting her forehead on her hand, covering her eyes, wishing she could hide from the answer she already knew. The pain would continue until she had the courage to do what she should have done at the start. It was both as simple—and as hard—as that!

'Are you all right?'

Mari jumped because she'd hadn't heard O'Neil's return; when she took her hand away from her face, she saw that he had let Founder back in when he had come. Now the two of them were standing in the kitchen doorway, each regarding her with an expression of wary concern.

'Of course I'm all right. I've been thinking, that's all.'

'And . . .' O'Neil prompted, still wary.

'I'm not going to New York,' she announced firmly. Her decision was made and she was determined to make it stick. Still she avoided his gaze. 'I'm not going to see the doctor again. I appreciate your concern . . .' Such a bloodless, inadequate way to describe his caring, his closeness, his kindness, she acknowledged unhappily, even as she began again. 'But seeing the doctor won't do any good. Instead, I'm going to do what I ought to have done a long time ago, back before——' she hesitated, fighting the sudden unsteadiness in her voice, then forged on '—before we began to mean something to each other. Once, a long time ago, you promised that you'd leave if I ever wanted you to, if I began to think things were getting out of control. Well, things *are* out of control, and it's almost too late, but it's better now than some time later—when things would only be worse, and it would hurt even more. We're not in too deeply yet—I mean, it's not as though we've done anything . . . drastic. You'll forget about this, and it wasn't even what you wanted, at the start. It's better this way, so . . . O'Neil——' She paused once more, drawing a deep breath. 'Will you please go away now—for good?'

'No.'

'No?' she repeated, dumbfounded. 'What kind of an answer is that? You promised!'

'Things were different when I made that promise.' He spoke calmly enough, and appeared deceptively at ease. Only his hands, clenched into tight fists, gave any emotion away. 'It's all changed now, Mari. There's no going back.'

'But you *promised*,' she said again. 'You can't break your promise!'

'I can and I have. It's the first, and—I sincerely hope—the last time I'll break a promise to you, but I can't leave you now. I've fallen in love with you, and you claim to have fallen in love with me——'

'I *have* fallen in love with you,' she corrected firmly, 'which is why I want you to leave.'

'That makes no sense at all!'

'But it does, O'Neil. Don't you see? If you don't go now, things will get worse. We'll get more deeply involved—for whatever time there is left—and that will only make the hurt worse! It's not fair of me to put you through that, and I don't want something that makes me wish I had forever. I can't put us through that when we both know the outcome's inevitable.'

'We don't know that,' he pointed out mildly enough, but she could hear anger and frustration, only barely held in check. 'Mari, you haven't seen a doctor in five years; in that length of time, things are bound to have changed.'

'O'Neil,' she warned, 'we went through all this last night.'

'And you agreed.'

'I wasn't thinking straight last night. I really wasn't thinking at all. Damn it, O'Neil, *listen* to us! We're not friends any more. *This* is between us! We're not happy; we're fighting. We'll tear each other apart if you don't go away now!'

'Not until you've seen the doctor,' he objected stubbornly, his control beginning to fray. 'You can't possibly make this decision—do this to us—when you don't even know how things stand. And even if we find that nothing has changed, I'll still want to be with you until . . .'

'. . . until I die,' she supplied, filling the silence between them. Her emotional state had entered a new phase, she noted with one part of her mind. She felt curiously detached from what they were saying—the icy calm of resignation, she supposed. 'Won't that be fun for you? Waking up each morning to wonder if I'm still asleep, or if I died in the night, watching me all the time—the way you've been watching me this morning. No, O'Neil, it wouldn't be fair to you.'

'Let *me* be the judge of that!'

'And I'd hate it,' she continued, ignoring his interruption. 'Neither of us should have to live that way. O'Neil, why can't you just let it go?'

'Because you mean too much. Because I never

thought I'd feel this way again.' All this time, he had been standing in the doorway; now he eased on to the stool next to hers, turning to face her. 'I thought this was over for me—loving someone, caring. I was convinced that something inside me died when Jill did, and then I found you.' Carefully he took her hand in his, transmitting to her something of his gentle strength. 'I've told you before how I felt—that no one would ever matter to me again, but I was wrong. You *matter*, although it took me a while to admit it. I was falling in love with you from the start—prizing the time I spent with you, thinking about you the rest of the time, beginning to hate it when I had to be gone, hurrying my work, always thinking about how it would be when I got back to you. Love, you can't make me give all that up! Now that I've got you——'

'But you *haven't*,' she cried, snatching her hand away, clasping both tightly together, fighting for strength against the feeling in his voice. 'It can't last! O'Neil, I'm going to die!'

'No! I won't accept that!' With a quick, uneven movement he turned away from her to grip the edge of the counter so fiercely that his knuckles showed white. 'I can't accept it,' he continued savagely. 'This time, at least, there's a chance. I don't just have to stand there and wait!'

They were caught in a mad nightmare of raw emotion, and Mari sensed that there was more to this—more to what O'Neil was saying—than she knew. 'What do you mean?' she asked, and then with dawning comprehension, added, 'Is this about your wife?'

He shook his head, staring down at his hands. 'Never mind,' he said, sounding weary. 'I shouldn't have said it.'

'But you did, and you can't just let it drop.' Now it

was her turn to take his hands, turning him back to face her. 'O'Neil, tell me what this is all about.'

'When Jill died—a long story,' he answered at last, and she could sense the effort it took him to speak. 'I told you she died, but not the whole story. I've never told anyone the whole story, but I suppose you're entitled to know, to understand how I feel.'

He was silent for a long while—gathering his courage, Mari guessed, staring down at their joined hands, watching his thumb rub absently over her fingers. 'After we were married, she always travelled with me,' he began. 'Even when she was pregnant, she came with me—until the doctor said she should stay home until after the baby was born. We weren't living in the safest part of the city—I was just starting the firm and money was tight—so we decided to get her a guard dog to protect her when I was gone. It was really a joke, because she didn't want a mean dog, so we chose a cowardly one. He looked fierce enough and he could bark like mad, but he couldn't have attacked anyone if his life depended on it. What we forgot, of course, was that *her* life depended on that dog . . .

'I'd gone to Brazil to bid on a contract, and one night—as she was taking him out for a walk before bed—three men attacked her. They killed the dog and dragged Jill into an alley . . . and did unspeakable things. It was madness, drug-induced, I suppose, and——' He stopped abruptly, and when he resumed Mari could only guess at the details he was omitting in an effort to spare them both. 'They didn't kill her. The doctors tried that night to save the child, without success, and Jill survived nearly a year, but on life-support systems. They call it brain death, and there was nothing they could do, nothing I could do but watch, and try to comprehend how it could be happening . . . and then she died.

'But now—everything's changed.' O'Neil looked up to meet Mari's gaze for the first time since he had started his terrible story. 'It had been years, and the pain had pretty well receded, but I didn't think I'd ever be completely over it. Then I met you, and I came alive again, discovered that it's possible to fall in love twice.'

'And I had to ruin everything by telling you about my—my problem.'

'Damn it, you didn't ruin everything! Don't you see?' he demanded, leaning closer, his piercing blue gaze fixed on her face. 'Lord knows, I wish things were different, that we didn't have this to deal with, but that's just the point. We *can* deal with it, Mari! It's not like the last time, when nothing could be done, when all I could do was stand by and watch the inevitable happen.'

'Are you sure I'm not just a replacement?' Mari asked carefully, feeling her way into his volatile mix of past and present emotion. 'Are you trying for a happy ending now, when you couldn't have one before? Are you attracted to me, or to the idea of making things come out right this time?'

'If that were true, I wouldn't have declared myself before I ever knew there was a problem,' he pointed out reasonably, then managed a convincing smile. 'Besides, I'm not just attracted to you. I'm in love with you! What happened with Jill is important only because it's taught me just how precious this is, how much can be lost. Mari, love, it's such an incredible *gift*—to love and be loved, to be in this together, to know that we at least have a chance.'

'We don't know that,' she reminded him quickly, fighting the strength of his conviction, fighting to maintain that calm acceptance of the inevitable which had held her together for the last five years. 'The doctor didn't give me any chance at all.'

'But that was years ago. We don't know—we can't know—until we talk to this man again. For pity's sake, Mari, don't give up on yourself—on us—unless we're sure! Come to New York with me now, so that we can see this man. Give yourself, give *us* at least that much of a chance!'

How could she say no? she wondered wildly, feeling the last of her calm acceptance slip away. O'Neil had destroyed it with his gaze, his fierce grip on her hands, with the sheer vitality of his presence. With O'Neil, she could almost believe . . . 'All right,' she conceded at last, and he leaned closer, until their knees touched. Still perched on their stools, he drew her into a clumsy embrace. Needing his strength, Mari surrendered, slipping her arms around his waist and leaning her head on his chest.

For a moment they were still, holding each other fiercely, as though it would take nothing more to solve this problem. Then, with uncharacteristic jealousy, Founder insinuated himself between them, insistently demanding first O'Neil's attention and then hers.

'I forgot to give him his breakfast,' Mari explained, her voice muffled against O'Neil's shirt. Then, as the next logical thought struck her, she straightened up, breaking their embrace. 'If I go to New York, what about Founder? I suppose I'll have to leave him with Lily and Nate.' Distractedly, she ran a hand through her hair, dreading Lily's reaction when she heard about this trip to New York. 'He knows her and likes the kids; he'll be happier there than anywhere else.'

'I never thought I'd be jealous of a dog,' O'Neil observed with one of his slanted grins, watching as Mari got down from her stool to open a can of dog food, 'but I really can't be—not when he and I have so much in common.'

'What?'

'We were both strays,' he told her, getting to his feet and catching her by the shoulders to draw her close, 'and you took us both in.'

'And on the same day,' she supplied ruefully, and felt the soft rumble of his laughter. 'I didn't know what I was doing.'

'Yes, you did,' he teased, drawing her even closer. 'You'd finally decided to stop avoiding attachments. Those five years of simplicity and calm had begun to pale. You didn't want to be alone any longer, love, and neither did I. I needed you as much as poor Founder did, and you needed us. Didn't you, love?'

'I suppose I must have,' she admitted, looking up at his face, its planes and angles so well-known and—yes, so loved, she realised, reaching up to brush back the errant slant of hair on his forehead. 'Yes,' she finally said, because he had given her the courage to admit the truth. 'I did need you, O'Neil. I still do.'

'Ah! Thanks for that, darling Mari,' he told her, releasing the careful breath he'd been holding, 'and thanks to the trick of the wind that landed me in your meadow that first morning.' Then he kissed her with the same gentle conviction that had been sustaining her all morning, and for that moment, at least, she believed that there *were* happy endings, that O'Neil really did have the power to make things come out right this time.

CHAPTER SIX

'SO now the two of you are going off to New York together.' Reacting exactly as Mari had known she would, Lily glanced pointedly out of the kitchen window to where O'Neil waited behind the wheel of the Porsche. 'Are you already sleeping together, or do you intend to start in the big city?'

'It's not like that,' Mari objected crossly. 'O'Neil's taking me to New York because——' She stopped abruptly, because it was better to have Lily think that she and O'Neil were having an affair than to tell her the truth. 'Because I have to see someone there,' she finished lamely.

'I'll just bet,' Lily agreed grimly, then instantly reverted to her patented older-sisterly concern. 'Mari darling, don't do it! He's in love with you—he must be! The way he watched you, that day at the picnic—you're too close to see how he looks at you. And he's hung around most of the summer, hasn't he? Would he have kept coming back if he wasn't in love with you?'

'He *is* in love with me,' Mari said proudly. 'He told me so.'

'And you're in love with him too,' Lily observed gloomily, 'so in love with him that you're prepared to let him have the quick fix. Mari, don't you see what you're doing? You're letting him have you without the bother of getting married. Why should he buy the cow when he can get the milk free?'

'*Lily!*'

109

'Well, it's true, even if it doesn't sound very nice,' Lily admitted defensively. 'You can't blame me if my mind naturally runs to cows and milk. I do live on a dairy farm, you know, and *I* know that *is* what O'Neil is doing!'

'It's not! You don't understand,' Mari retorted, very much on her dignity. 'I have to go to New York on some business, and O'Neil is kind enough to take me there. We're not having an affair! In fact, we're thinking about getting married.'

'Of course he'd mention marriage,' Lily agreed, now worldly-wise—although how she could even pretend to be wordly-wise when she had never so much as gone out with anyone but Nate, Mari didn't know. 'He's clever enough to know when he's got to dangle the carrot.'

'You're mixing your metaphors, Lily,' Mari said coolly, beginning to edge towards the door.

'I'm upset! I'm worried about you, darling.'

'And I'm twenty-nine—surely too old to need worrying about.'

'But——'

'But nothing!' Mari had suddenly had more than she could take, to be talking about this when she and O'Neil were facing so much. 'If you'd rather not keep Founder, I can find someone else.'

'Of course we'll keep Founder. Don't be an idiot, Mari.' Instantly contrite, Lily gave her a quick hug. 'And don't be angry with me that I worry. I can't help it. It's——'

'I know—the habit of a lifetime,' Mari finished for her, and they both laughed a little unsteadily. 'It's just that after a lifetime of being me, I think I can take care of myself.'

'But you're still such an innocent, such a babe in the woods.'

'Who lived in New York—Sin City, USA, by your standards—for six years,' Mari reminded her. 'Did it ever occur to you that I might have known O'Neil way back then? For all you know, we might already have had a flaming affair.'

'Did you?' demanded Lily, instantly diverted. 'Did you know him? Did you have an affair? Is that why he suddenly came up here and——'

'Of course not! That was a joke, Lily, and I don't have time for another round of twenty questions.'

'All right—I'm sorry.' Lily held up her hands in a gesture of surrender. 'And don't worry about Founder; we'll take good care of him. And—have fun, if that's what I ought to say in the circumstances.'

Mari, kneeling to give Founder a last hug, ignored the comment. Instead she got to her feet, called her thanks over her shoulder, and fled to the car.

'You look grim,' O'Neil observed as he started the engine and reversed out of the drive. 'What happened in there?'

'Lily was her usual big-sisterly self,' Mari explained darkly. 'She's afraid that you're taking me off to have an affair, and she was advising me to hold out for marriage.'

'Lord, she got that one wrong,' said O'Neil with a laugh bordering on bitterness. 'Backwards, in fact. And she should have been a little more interested in what we hope to find out about you.'

'She doesn't know about that. I didn't tell her.'

'Why not?' he asked with a quick glance. 'Didn't you want to tell her until we've got some good news?'

'No. It's that she doesn't know anything about any of this. None of them do.'

'For pity's sake, Mari!' O'Neil applied the brakes, and stopped the car dead in the deserted country road so that he could turn to look directly at her. 'Do you mean that you've never told anyone about this? That you've spent the last five years *entirely* alone with this?'

'Well . . . yes,' she admitted uncomfortably, trapped by his gaze. 'I couldn't.'

'But *why*? It's not natural!'

'It is, if you consider what my family is like! They're wonderful people, but they worry so about me, and they never let go. You don't know what it's like to have all those people worrying about you because you're the youngest and they're sure you haven't grown up yet and that you're incapable of taking care of yourself.'

'I begin to think they may be right,' O'Neil said grimly, then reached across to put his hand over hers. 'At least you've got me now, and as soon as we get this thing straightened out you're going to tell them what you ought to have told them five years ago. Dear heaven!' He shook his head, removed his hand long enough to get the car started again, then took her nervously twisting hands in one of his again. 'It's a good thing you've got me now,' he said again, and Mari could only nod, grateful for his comforting touch.

'I'm so glad you live here!' Mari exclaimed when they reached O'Neil's city home on a quiet side street at the fringe of Greenwich Village. It had been mid-afternoon when they had arrived in New York, but already the traffic had been building to its rush-hour peak. In the years of her absence, the city had grown more crowded, Mari thought, busier and noisier, with many new tall structures on the skyline. She hadn't quite dared to believe that a neighbourhood like O'Neil's had survived, this tree-lined oasis of mellowed brick three and four-storey town houses.

'I lived not far away, but in a high-rise on a busy street. I used to dream of living in a place like this.' she confided approvingly, studying O'Neil's house while he searched his pockets for his keys. It was old, built about 1820, she guessed, three storeys of soft red brick and small-paned windows. Granite steps led up to the freshly painted black front door, its brass knocker and door latch a glittering contrast. 'It's beautiful!'

'Better not pass judgement until you've seen the inside,' O'Neil cautioned as he opened the door. 'It's different, and you may not like it.'

'Different' was putting it mildly, Mari saw as soon as she stepped inside to find herself in one vast space. There were no rooms in the conventional sense; instead, the main floor living-area was completely open, extending up to the flat roof, interrupted only by two partial levels, one and two storeys above. Three walls were of exposed brick, while the fourth—the garden wall—appeared to be one huge sheet of glass set between structural steel beams.

'What on earth did you do?' she demanded, turning back to him. 'Totally gut this poor old house?'

'I'm not quite such a philistine as that,' he chided, smiling apologetically. 'I bought it after it had been pretty well destroyed by a fire. The front façade was left, and the two walls separating it from its neighbours, but all the interior partitions were gone and the back wall had been so badly damaged that it was falling down. Most people thought there was nothing to do but complete the destruction—take out everything that was left, like a rotten tooth—but I thought it would be a shame to interject a modern note on an old street like this. So I managed to save the façade, and then did as I pleased behind it.'

'Well, it's not bad, I suppose,' Mari said doubtfully, looking around once more. 'At least it's something you chose—not like the place in Vermont you grafted yourself on to. Still . . .' she hesitated, intimidated by all the open space and soaring height, '. . . it takes a little getting used to.'

'Then explore, why don't you?' He put down her suitcase, glancing briefly at his watch. 'There's time to call your doctor and set up an appointment for tomorrow. I'll do that now, if you'll give me his name.'

'Maristkas. John Maristkas.' She spelled the name.

'Right—I'll call now. Just wander, Mari,' he added absently, already looking through the telephone directory for the doctor's number.

Deliberately, Mari distanced herself from O'Neil and his call. She didn't want to be reminded—any more than she already had been!—of why she was here. It had been easy enough to ignore the reality while she had been noting the changes in the city and discovering where O'Neil lived. In fact, she'd been remembering that once she had liked New York, that in spite of its congestion and noise it had always held a kind of gritty excitement for her.

O'Neil's place now served as her distraction, and she felt that it might just be the best of all possible worlds—if she could only get used to all this space! Refusing to allow the soft insistence of O'Neil's words to penetrate her concentration, she found herself reflecting that in this quiet backwater street, with the green of a garden just beyond the wall of windows, she might once again find herself enjoying life in the city. Strange as it was, this reconstructed shell of a house appealed to her aesthetic sensibilities, just as the odd combination of furnishings appealed to the nonconformist in her.

Here the comfortably shabby, the sleekly modern and the best of antiques had been joined in a setting so unconventional that it seemed to demand that the rules of period and style be broken. Thoroughly absorbed

now, she ran her hand over the top of a wonderfully
intricate marquetry desk which shared a large and
threadbare Oriental rug with a grouping of equally well-
worn leather couches and chairs. On one brick wall, an
antique pine cupboard displayed a collection of African
pottery and ritual masks—things O'Neil had collected
on his travels, she supposed.

Beyond, open steps led to the upper levels, and she
took the stairs slowly, pausing to admire a series of pen-
and-ink sketches. They were careful renderings of scenes
of New York, she saw—the spare economy of the World
Trade Centre, the Gothic exuberance of a Fifth Avenue
mansion, the crowded confusion of Chinatown, even the
quiet serenity of this street, the façade of O'Neil's own
house nearly indistinguishable from the others. His own
work, she guessed, the precision of the work reminding
her of his handwriting on the postcard he had sent.

The second level, its small-paned windows
overlooking the street, was obviously a work-space,
spare and unadorned. There was a large work-table,
twin to the one at his place in Vermont, even to the
inevitable computer terminal. Against the low wooden
railing separating this space from the room below was a
larger drawing-board flanked by two gunmetal-grey
filing cabinets. On one wall, a daybed slip-covered in no-
nonsense grey was set between two tables piled high
with what appeared to be technical journals and books.
Near the stairs, she cautiously opened a closed door,
finding nothing more interesting than a simple bath and
empty closet area.

The open steps traversed back across the wall to reach
the larger third level—O'Neil's bedroom, dominated by
an enormous, elaborately carved Victorian bed and a
matching *armoire* on the opposite wall. Beside the bed, a
table held more books and magazines, but otherwise

the space was empty. Visual impact was provided by the wall of windows overlooking the garden and the ornate balustrade over which one could look down a dizzying thirty feet to the main floor.

'You've got as far as my bedroom, I see.' Only when he called up to her did Mari realise that O'Neil had finished his telephone call. Now he came up the stairs, his long legs taking them two at a time. 'I hope you like it reasonably well,' he continued as he joined her. 'You'll be sleeping here—alone, if you like,' he added when he saw her quick, doubtful expression.

'Have you seen the bathroom?' he continued smoothly, giving her no time to express any qualms. 'It's my particular pride.'

'I can see why,' she agreed when she had followed him into that room, grateful for an excuse to avoid lingering on the subject of sleeping accommodation. In the centre of the room was a huge old-fashioned ball-and-claw-footed tub; the basin was set into an ornately carved marble-topped cabinet; even the toilet was an elaborately detailed antique, complete with overhead tank and shining brass pull-chain. 'Where on earth did you find these things?'

'In an old mansion about to be torn down, and I was lucky to get them,' O'Neil explained with a self-satisfied smile. 'These things are collectors' items, you know. When ones as good as these come on the market, the competition can be fierce.'

'I'm sure,' she agreed with mock gravity, then spoiled it with a fit of giggles. 'I'm sorry, but if you could hear how you sound! Fierce competition over toilets and bathtubs . . . O'Neil, you've got unexpected depths. You're not quite as detached and high-tech as I thought. This bathroom's a revolt against all that, and the bedroom too. I wouldn't have expected you to buy anything old for yourself, but there's quite a bit. All good too,' she added as they started back down the stairs. 'You've got a good eye. You did those, didn't you?' she asked, indicating the pen-and-ink sketches.

'I'm afraid so. They're not art, of course——'

'But they are!' Mari paused to study more closely the one of Chinatown. 'Really very good. Even if I didn't know you, I think I'd be able to tell that they were done by an engineer—someone whose roots are in drafting—but they're nicely composed and this one in particular has nice energy and a lot of feeling You're a Renaissance man, O'Neil.'

'Hardly that,' he protested, but she knew he was pleased with the compliment and enjoyed being drawn out about things like the marquetry desk, the antique cupboard and the masks. With considerable enthusiasm and feeling, he described how and why he had acquired all the odd and unusual things in his house. Finally, when his recital was done, he offered an apologetic smile. 'Have I bored you to death?'

'Of course not! You've simply proved my point that you're a Renaissance man, and something of a romantic too.'

'But you already knew—or should have—that I'm a romantic,' he teased. 'Haven't I declared my undying love for you?'

'But I might not have believed you, if I hadn't seen this place. There's no *you* in the one in Vermont.'

'Oh, well.' He gestured dismissively. 'That was simply intended to be a base for ballooning in the summer and skiing in the winter. It wasn't supposed to mean anything, and it wouldn't, if it weren't for the fact that you live just over the ridge—at the moment. When we're married, you can move in with me. You can keep your place as a studio, if you like, but it's not really big enough for the two of us—to say nothing of how crowded it will be when we start a family, which we'd better do before your biological clock runs down. You do want a family, don't you?'

'No! Please . . .' She had borne more of this than she could take, and now she turned quickly away, her hands clasped tightly together, pressing against the sudden pain in the region of her heart. 'O'Neil, you're tempting fate! Don't plan for the future when I don't know if I have one.'

'But you will; you'll see.' His arms came around her, drawing her back against the line of his body, his hands covering hers. 'And it won't be long until you hear. We're going to see the doctor tomorrow noon. I talked directly to him and he remembered you; he wondered why you hadn't come back in all this time.'

'He probably had his secretary find my record,' Mari objected, staring down, watching the way his hands were holding hers. He had been doing that all day, she realised—holding her hands, sharing his strength with her. 'And I know you, O'Neil,' she continued after a moment. 'If the doctor is seeing us so soon, it's only because you never take no for an answer. You never give up until you've gotten your own way.'

'That's right, and this time's no different, but I don't believe the doctor has given up on you. I'm nothing to him, so there's no reason for him to do what I want unless he thinks there's some purpose in seeing you.'

'You intimidated him, or else he's just curious.' This time, however, her objection was more form than substance, she noted. Whatever it was O'Neil could do to her, he was doing it once again. The cold knot of fear was nearly gone now and, while she didn't precisely *believe*, she wasn't quite so unbelieving as she had been a few minutes before.

'Better now?' she heard O'Neil whisper, his lips very close to her ear. She supposed he had felt—as she had—the tension leaving her. She was leaning quite naturally against him now, and her fingers had unconsciously laced themselves through his.

'I suppose I am,' she admitted grudgingly, 'although I don't know why. You've gotten your own way again. And again,' she added when he somehow contrived to turn her to face him, his arms still around her.

'You said it—I always get my way,' he told her, his voice deeper and a little rough, his lips just a few tantalising inches from her own.

'And now I suppose you want me to kiss you?'

'If you like,' he allowed with a lazy smile, 'although what I had in mind was to kiss you.'

'We could meet half-way,' she suggested, linking her arms around his neck, rewarded by his quick expression of pleasure, possibly even gratitude or relief.

Then she gave up trying to think, as they shared a kiss unlike any she'd known before. All she was sure of was that there was more than passion or need in this joining. There was depth, understanding, the need to be close in their caring, the desire to forget all the fear and uncertainty, a wanting to be safe, to belong . . .

'I think,' O'Neil finally managed, his voice sounding ragged, his breathing at least as erratic as hers, 'that we'd better find something else to do, before the issue of who sleeps where becomes a moot one.' He stepped back a pace, shoving his hands in his pockets. 'Let's go for a walk,' he suggested a little more firmly. 'We can work up an appetite for dinner—and kill the other appetite that seems to have developed between us. You said you lived near here. Why don't you show me?'

They walked for more than two hours, through the twilight and into the night. After their brief stop outside the nondescript apartment block which had been Mari's home for most of her time in the city, they managed to explore much of Greenwich Village. To Mari, it was a curious paradox of the well remembered and the amazingly fresh and new. Washington Square, McDougal Street, Greenwich Avenue, the honeycomb of little streets to the west—they were all more alive than she'd remembered, and even the garishly commerical sections had a strange kind of beauty and vitality.

'It's not much like Vermont, which may be why I'm enjoying it so,' she admitted reluctantly when they had finally stopped for dinner in a little French restaurant near the end of O'Neil's street. 'It's the contrast, I suppose, but I could almost say that I've missed it.'

'Then why not say it?' O'Neil asked with the same expression of indulgent amusement with which he had been regarding her all evening. 'There's nothing wrong with saying that you miss a place where you spent several years of your life. Or are you afraid that saying it will be an admission that you made a mistake in leaving?'

'No, it's not that. Leaving wasn't a mistake. It was *time* to leave—not just because of the sparrow, or because things had suddenly changed for me. Already, before those things happened, I'd started spending too much of my time trying to find places with trees and grass.'

'You can take the girl out of Vermont,' he began with a teasing smile, and they finished together, 'but you can't take Vermont out of the girl.'

'And you, O'Neil, have the best of all possible worlds,' she continued expansively between bites of Dover sole—'Sole *Anglaise*', the resolutely French menu called it—and sips of a fine white wine. 'You get to divide your time between New York and Vermont.'

'With the occasional side trip to some of the hottest and dustiest parts of the world thrown in for good measure.'

'True,' she conceded, 'but those side trips must just make you appreciate the other two all the more.'

'These last few months, all the trips have done is make me appreciate *you* all the more.'

'But still,' she persisted, determined to keep him to the subject, 'you can live in my two favourite places. I envy you.'

'No need to envy me,' he countered quickly. 'Just marry me, and we can share this best of all possible worlds.'

'Oh, well . . .' She smiled uncertainly, waiting for his words to destroy her mood of pleasant contentment, waiting to feel fear at the way he was tempting fate again. When nothing happened, she could only conclude that the effects of good food and wine had succeeded in insulating her from the sharper edges of reality. At the moment, the thought of being married to O'Neil, of living in New York and Vermont—or anywhere else, so long as they were together—seemed infinitely appealing. Even possible, she discovered with a feeling of unexpected optimism, then forced herself to concentrate on what he was saying.

'I mention marriage, and for once I don't hear any objection. That's promising, Mari. We seem to be making some progress.'

'Perhaps we are, unless it's just that I'm too muddled to give your idea the thought it deserves.' Nor did she want to, she told herself. Thinking meant worrying and being afraid . . . No, she didn't want to think right now, she concluded, only partially successful in smothering a yawn.

'You're tired. We'll go home.'

Home, Mari repeated to herself while O'Neil summoned the waiter and settled the bill. That had a lovely ring to it—the way O'Neil had said, 'We'll go home.' Still preoccupied with the idea of home and O'Neil, she permitted him to guide her out of the restaurant. Once on the street, she stood passively, waiting for him to show her which way to go.

'Poor girl, you're out on your feet,' she heard him say, and felt his arm around her shoulders, propelling her forward, his long stride reduced to match her shorter, slower steps. Only when they were back inside the house did he release her to turn the dead bolt on the door. 'We should have eaten sooner,' he apologised, 'and I shouldn't have made you do so much walking.'

'Oh, no, I enjoyed it. Loved every minute of it, if you want the truth.' Not waiting to see if he intended to kiss her, Mari took a step forward and leaned against him, slipping her arms around his neck. 'I can't remember when I've been as happy as I have been this evening, as I am right now. Which is strange,' she continued after a moment, when he didn't speak. 'I ought to be worrying about that appointment tomorrow. I expect I am, somewhere underneath, but I don't feel it.

'You keep it away, O'Neil,' she confided, resting her head on his shoulder, feeling safe and contented when his arms came around her, drawing her closer still. 'It doesn't make any sense that you keep it away, because you're the one who made it all come back when I was doing so well at keeping it out of my mind. Because of you, I should be more afraid, but I'm not . . . I think.

Do you suppose that's because I love you so much?'

'I'm not sure, love.'

'Neither am I. I'm confused.' She sighed, her grip on him involuntarily tightening. 'I think you're the only thing holding me together right now. Without you, I might fall apart. You're the only courage I've got right now. O'Neil, kiss me,' she said with sudden urgency, lifting her face to his. 'Please kiss me.'

'How could I not?' he asked with a twisted smile.

When his mouth closed over hers, she strained closer, tangling her fingers in his thick hair, revelling in his instant hunger which matched hers. I *need* this, she thought, coherence slipping away, consumed by the slow, stirring flame of passion and a fierce joy. This is *real*! This is belonging and sharing and all the things I want just as much as he does . . .

'Mari, love,' he murmured an infinity later, when their kiss had finally ended, 'let me be with you tonight.'

She wanted that more than anything, *needed* to be with him . . . but there was something wrong with the idea. 'I don't think we should,' she answered slowly, sorting through her thoughts. 'I've been using you all day, and if you stay with me tonight, I'll just be using you again.'

'Then use me, love,' he breathed, his lips teasing at hers. 'Lord, I'm not complaining!'

Why not? she asked herself, trying hard to concentrate and failing miserably when his lips continued their clever work. To be with him would feel so good and mean so much. Oh, hell, she thought despairingly, reality finally cutting through all the confusion. 'No. We can't, O'Neil.'

'Why not, for Pete's sake?'

'Because that's too easy, and not fair to either of us—

not when we still don't know if we've got any future.'

'We *do* have a future,' he said savagely, not angry with her, but with fate. 'I refuse to accept anything else!'

'O'Neil, this may come as a shock to you,' she began, wondering that she was able to find some humour, even in a moment like this, 'but there are some things that even you can't control, and I'm afraid that my future is one of them. I may not have one.'

'Then all the more reason to take what we *do* have!'

'All the more reason not to, you *should* mean,' she corrected kindly. 'Don't you see? If we both do what we're wanting to, then we'll have something *real* to lose. Loving each other is abstract, but making love would be something real that could be taken away.'

'If you think that loving you isn't real——'

'Well, perhaps, but not quite *as* real.'

'Every bit as real, believe me. Making love is no different from loving!'

'For you, perhaps, but not for *me*! Don't ask this of me, O'Neil! I've been thinking about this thing of mine for years, deciding what I can do without, what I can bear to leave. I think, if I have to, I can handle leaving behind what I have now—even you. But this! If I share this part of loving with you—if I finally understand what it *is*, what it means—I don't think I could bear to leave it behind.'

'All right, I understand,' he finally conceded, even managing a smile, 'but when we see the doctor tomorrow—when you find out that you do have a future, that you don't have to leave anything behind— you're going to remember tonight and feel like a bloody fool. And when we finally do make love, and it's as good as I know it will be between us—you're going to wonder why you were such an idiot as to refuse to do it sooner.'

'If you say so,' she agreed demurely, adopting his light approach because, after all, it probably was the easiest way to handle this. 'I'll even let you rub it in, if you like. You may say "I told you so" as many times as you like.'

'I probably will, but not for long,' he assured her, teasing now. 'I'll be too busy—finding other and infinitely more interesting things to say and do. There won't be much time for "I told you so".'

They laughed then, making it into a kind of joke, but Mari could no longer see the humour when she found herself alone in O'Neil's huge Victorian bed. Then there was nothing left but loneliness and the painful awareness of O'Neil alone on the daybed one level down. No walls separated them, Mari mused, lying awake in the darkness. There was nothing between them but space and a flight of stairs . . .

And her fears, she reminded herself, knowing how easy it would have been to forget her fears, or at least ignore them for one night. But that would be a mistake, if tomorrow the doctor had nothing new to say. If that happened, then she and O'Neil would have had one night of learning to be together—just when they would have to learn to be alone again.

CHAPTER SEVEN

'AH, yes. Miss Scott. I'm pleased to see you again. And Mr O'Neil, of course. We spoke yesterday. Why don't you both come in and sit down?' Dr Maristkas ushered them into his private office, and with impersonal solicitude saw that Mari was seated.

He hadn't changed, she saw, watching him as he resumed his place behind his impressive desk. He'd been a middle-aged and remote figure five years ago; now he looked no older and was just as remote, not looking at her as he carefully squared the placement of the file folder before him. Mine, she thought with a sense of detachment, ignoring O'Neil's impatient shift in the chair beside hers. There was no sense trying to hurry Dr Maristkas. She knew from five years ago that his words had a life of their own. They would wind a slow and ponderous course—even when a death sentence was all they could offer.

'Well, Miss Scott,' he began now, looking across his desk at her, 'I was surprised, frankly, when Mr O'Neil told me that no doctor had been following you during the last five years.'

Surprised that I was still alive would be more like it, Mari told herself, willing her hands to be still, forcing herself to sit calmly while he finished his visual inspection of her. She had been playing this kind of game all morning, and O'Neil had been playing the same kind of game—each of them pretending a calm neither was feeling, each pretending that this was a normal and commonplace day. 'I didn't think there

126

was any point in seeing another doctor,' she offered when she realised that Dr Maristkas was waiting for some response from her. 'You seemed pretty definite about your findings. Unequivocal, even.'

'Well, yes, I'm sure it seemed that way to you.' Dr Maristkas looked down, making a careful tent of his fingers, touching the tip of each of its mirror image. 'In fact, it seemed that way to me, at the time. A malformation in that area of the brain was considered inoperable—five years ago. But the whole point of medicine, Miss Scott, is that things don't stay the same. What is considered untreatable today may be highly amenable to treatment in five years' time. Had you been followed by any reputable neurologist during the last five years, he would undoubtedly have made you aware of the progress in neuro-surgical techniques during that time.'

O'Neil, who had been motionless beside her since Dr Maristkas began to speak, stirred slightly. When Mari glanced in his direction, she saw his quick look of triumph, a piercing expression of 'I told you so'.

'As it happens,' Dr Maristkas resumed, studying the structure he had made of his fingers, 'there has been quite dramatic progress in the field. One of my colleagues—Saul Horner, here in New York—has made a considerable contribution to the field. In fact, he has had remarkable success in surgery on that part of the brain in which your problem lies.'

'Yes?' Mari waited, hardly daring to breathe—certainly not daring to hope!—while the doctor rearranged the placement of his fingers.

'Had *I* been following you,' he explained with only the slightest hint of reproof in his voice, 'I would have referred you to Dr Horner at least two years ago. I certainly think you should see him now. Yesterday, after I spoke with Mr O'Neil, I took the liberty of discussing your case with Dr Horner. He's very eager to see you. In fact, he *will* see you late this afternoon—unless you object.'

'No . . .' Mari began tentatively, not entirely sure she was grasping the implications of what Dr Maristkas had said. Then, as O'Neil shot her a compelling look, she pulled herself together and continued more firmly, 'No, of course not, if you think I should.'

'There's no doubt in my mind, Miss Scott.' Dr Maristkas abandoned the contemplation of his fingers to look directly at her once more. 'This is a possibility you certainly ought to explore. You'd be a fool not to.'

'What did I *tell* you?' O'Neil demanded as soon as he had closed the office door behind them. He turned, seizing her arms in an iron grip, staring down at her, the fierce glitter of triumph still in his eyes. 'I *told* you things could have changed! You'll see. We're going to lick this thing, and everything's going to be fine!'

'But——' Mari hesitated, needing to be sensible, but hating to burst his bubble. 'We can't be sure. Nothing's certain yet.'

'But it will be—very soon.' His fingers bit into her arms. 'For pity's sake, Mari, try to show a little enthusiasm!'

'I wish I could, but it's still too new.'

'Of course—I should have realised that.' He was instantly contrite. 'Poor girl! I've known about this for less than two days, and you've been living with it for years.' Oblivious to the curious stares of people passing in the hallway, he folded her into his arms. 'I'm sorry, love,' he apologised. 'I suppose, at the moment, this means more to me than to you. You've been living with what you thought was a certainty, but when you hit me with the news, all I could think was that *this time* there was a chance. And now, to know that I'm right—well, you can't know how much that means to me. In time, it will come to mean just as much to you. You'll begin to get used to the idea, and then you'll *believe*—just as strongly as I do!'

If Dr Maristkas was too ponderously slow for Mari's taste, Dr Horner proved to be a vivid contrast—young and enthusiastically direct.

'What a treat you are,' he began the moment Mari and O'Neil were admitted to his office, fixing Mari with his lively stare. 'I usually don't find people like you until it's too late—or nearly so. Tell me,' he continued, peering down at what Mari suspected was her file from Dr Maristkas's office, probably sent over by messenger, 'are you really *Marigold* Scott?'

'I'm afraid so,' she admitted, already charmed, liking his intensity, 'but if you plan to call me by my first name, I prefer Mari.'

'What are you? One of those poor kids whose parents didn't stop to think whether or not you'd like the name you were given?' Unlike Dr Maristkas, he hadn't removed himself to sit behind his desk. Instead, he was perched on the front corner, directly in front of Mari and O'Neil, and now he grinned engagingly at both of them. 'Just remember that when you two have children of your own,' he advised. 'Give their names a little more thought.'

When *we* have children, Mari thought with a slight shiver of combined optimism and dread. Surely this man—who held her fate in his hands at this moment—wouldn't say such a thing unless . . .

'—beside the point, right now,' Dr Horner was saying now, and Mari forced herself to put aside the delicious thought of the children she and O'Neil might have. 'I said you were a treat,' Dr Horner continued, 'but do you have any idea what a treat you are—or at least could be?'

'Er . . . no.'

'Well, you've got a unique medical problem. In the general population, your type of venous defect is exceedingly rare, and it's even more uncommon to find someone known to have it before it gives way. Did Dr Maristkas explain the consequences when this happens?'

'There didn't seem much to explain,' Mari offered. 'He said it was invariably fatal.'

'Not invariably,' Dr Horner corrected quickly. 'At least, there's no reason why it should be *now*. It was, of course, at the time he made your initial diagnosis. What you've got is a time-bomb of sorts, ticking away in your head, and at your age, the fuse is getting too short. If the bomb goes off, a great deal of damage will be done—damage that will most likely kill you.

'Now,' he continued, warming to the subject, clearly unaware that his listeners—who, after all, had a more personal stake in the matter—might find his unadorned explanation hard to hear, 'to complicate things further, your time-bomb—the vessel with the defect—is in a part of the brain difficult to reach through surgery. In the past, getting to that vessel meant going through—and damaging—other parts of the brain, which only made a bad situation worse. What you need is a surgical procedure that will permit the repair of the defective vessel, and one that won't damage other parts of the brain.

'And that's what I've got,' he stated with obvious pride. 'I've got a new approach—I take a different path in to the vessel, one which reduces the possibility of damage. This new approach, combined with new instruments and equipment, has the potential to reduce the damage to something within acceptable limits—something close to nil. I've used this technique on a number of cases during the last three years, but all I've ever been able to do is prevent death. The vessel—in every case—had already let go, considerable damage had already been done, and my technique can't reverse damage—only prevent it.

'What makes you such a treat,' he continued, fixing his attention on Mari, 'is that you're a healthy young woman—or at least you were when you saw Dr Maristkas five years ago. If you're still healthy, and if the defect is where Dr Maristkas reports it to be, then you'd be an excellent candidate for my technique—the first I've ever had. *That's* what makes you potentially so special. I'd dearly love to try my technique on someone before the damage is done, and I think you just might be that person. It's an enormously exciting prospect.'

'For you, perhaps,' O'Neil said sharply, taking Mari's hand, his grip unexpectedly fierce, 'but it sounds to me as though she'd be nothing more than your guinea-pig.'

'Absolutely,' Dr Horner agreed unrepentantly, 'but that doesn't change the fact that I could be her salvation. Without me, she really doesn't have a chance, so what I'd like to do is admit her to my unit this evening. In fact, I've already made arrangements to have her admitted, if she's willing. There would be several days of testing before any decision could be made. Only if all the test results were good would we decide that she could have the surgery. Then it would be her turn to decide if she wanted it. Until then, I don't need a firm commitment from her, because I

may yet find that she's not an appropriate candidate
for my technique.'

'But if she is?' O'Neil probed, approaching the
matter with an engineer's logic. Emotion had been left
behind as he absorbed the data given; now he wanted
the bottom line, and Mari suspected that he had
completely forgotten her hand, still resting in his. 'If
she *is* an appropriate candidate for your technique,
what are her chances?'

'Very good, I'd say,' Dr Horner answered easily,
responding to O'Neil's approach. Two men of
science, Mari thought with a sense of panicky
bitterness, because the two of them were actually
comfortable in this technical realm where facts
mattered more than emotion. 'In the cases I've
operated on, I've done very little damage in addition
to what was already present; nor have I lost a patient.
I see no reason why the outcome should be any
different in this case—except, of course, that there
wouldn't be any damage to begin with, so long as we
do the surgery before the vessel blows.'

I've become a case, Mari thought despairingly, even
as O'Neil turned, fixing her with his triumphant gaze.
'So you see?' he demanded, and she could only nod
obediently. 'Then you'll proceed with the testing,'
O'Neil continued, switching his attention back to Dr
Horner. 'It's settled.'

'Not quite,' Dr Horner cautioned, belatedly
remembering Mari. 'Before we can proceed with the
tests, I need some sense that you're prepared to
consider surgery. There's no point in wasting my time
or taking up space in one of the beds in my unit if you
aren't willing to consider carrying this to the logical
conclusion. What do you say?'

'Mari?' O'Neil prompted when she didn't speak,

and she felt again the strength of his grip on her hand, the absolute and unshakeable strength of his conviction. 'You will, won't you? If Dr Horner says the surgery will work for you, you will have it done?'

'Yes, of course,' she answered automatically, her mind busy with another, deeper subject. This, she had suddenly discovered, was what love was about. It was going where you hadn't thought to go, where you were afraid to go. Like going up in a hot-air balloon, she told herself, remembering an early summer evening. Love was sometimes doing something terrifying because someone suddenly mattered so much to you that you found yourself compelled to ignore all your doubts and fears. And perhaps, like that early summer evening, the results this time would be just as good. 'Of course,' she said again, more firmly, smiling for O'Neil, trying to be brave, trying to hide the doubts and fears she hadn't yet quite mastered.

She spent the next few days submerged in the clinical routine of the hospital. She endured without complaint the endless questions, the poking and prodding, the numerous tests which ranged from the simple to the arcane, from the completely painless to the acutely uncomfortable. Through it all, she tried to ignore the fear gnawing at her, and she succeeded until the day Dr Horner finally spoke to her.

Until that afternoon, she'd seen nothing of him. Resident doctors and technicians were the ones who performed the various tests; Dr Horner had remained a remote and god-like figure, mentioned but never seen until he stopped briefly in her room after the second day of tests.

'I hear that you're an extraordinarily healthy young

woman—and a very good patient,' he told her, looking so pleased that Mari could almost feel his anticipation at the prospect of trying his procedure on her. 'You do what you're told and you don't complain, which is what we all like—a co-operative patient.'

'Well, I don't see that I've got much choice,' Mari was stung to reply. 'Besides, I want it over with as soon as possible. Not just the tests, but the whole business.'

'Wanting what comes after?' he asked cheerfully. 'Looking forward to being given the rest of your life?'

'It's more a case of dreading——'

'Well, don't get your hopes up just yet,' he advised, cutting her off, not even pretending to hear what she had tried to say. 'We've established that you're in such good shape that there's no reason to think that you couldn't withstand the surgery, but we've got to wait for the tests that will locate the malformation precisely. Whether or not we can even consider surgery will depend on location. Time will tell,' he finished casually, ducking quickly out of her room.

Easy for him to be casual, Mari thought bitterly, staring after him, resenting everything about his attitude. For him, her condition was merely an issue of academic interest. She represented nothing more to him than another first, a chance to add an impressive notch to his already impressive reputation. It's not *your* life that's at stake, she told the empty doorway. *I'm* the one who stands to lose everything, to lose even more than I ever thought I could have.

'I'm frightened,' she confessed to O'Neil when he came to visit that evening, laden with magazines, flowers, a pile of books. 'I'm terrified, if you want the truth.'

'Why? What happened?' he demanded, unceremoniously dumping everything into a chair and coming to sit beside her on the edge of the bed. 'Did something go wrong today?'

'No, it's nothing like that, nothing specific. It's just that I've got so much to lose,' she tried to explain, repeating the refrain that had been pounding in her head since Dr Horner's brief visit. 'So much more than there used to be,' she continued, her voice beginning to waver as O'Neil drew her into his arms.

'It was all so much easier before you came along,' she confided, her voice muffled against his shirt. 'Not nearly as nice, so I'm not complaining, but it *was* easier. All I had was a tidy little existence, and no one to mind terribly much when I checked out.'

'Your family,' O'Neil pointed out. 'Lord knows, they're protective enough of you.'

Mari shook her head. 'Oh, I know they worry about me, but they've always done that. It's become force of habit by now, even if it still bugs the hell out of me. Hell, can you imagine what they'd all make of this?' she demanded, briefly diverted by the idea. 'I was always a sickly child, catching every bug going around, but they were all just the usual childhood things—nothing to really worry about, even though they all did. Perhaps because she knew I was the last, Mother worried more about me, and that made everyone else worry more. They'd have a field day worrying about this mess! I'd have all of them standing around this bed, wringing their hands and fretting, but,' she continued more slowly, reality intruding once more, 'if it didn't end well—if the surgery couldn't be done, or if it did get done and ended badly . . . well, they'd get over it pretty quickly. When you look at it objectively—and I always have—they've all got their own lives, and I'm not

terribly important to any of them. Even my parents—I
mean, they've got four other children, after all.'

'Mari, they wouldn't feel that way!'

'Even so, they'd survive, but that's not really the
biggest point. It's that *I* didn't mind so terribly much
if I checked out early. I was liking my life, enjoying it
and doing exactly what I wanted to do, but it didn't
matter too awfully much. I'd gotten myself——' she
was crying now, feeling her tears being absorbed by
O'Neil's immaculate white shirt '—trained myself,
perhaps, not to care, to be willing to let go whenever
the time came. And then you happened, and you
matter so much. And that makes it so bad, because I
can't bear to think of losing what you mean to me, or
what it seems that I mean to you.'

'You don't need to, love! That's just the
point—there's a chance now.'

'But that just makes it worse,' she wailed, as five
years of emotion repressed suddenly welled to the
surface. 'Now, to be so close to a future, and just to
know that it's going to be snatched away——'

'But it's not, love,' O'Neil said sharply, speaking to
his fears as well as her own. 'This time, the surgery
will work. I believe it, and you should too.'

'But I can't! I've spent too many years not
believing, too many years knowing there wasn't a
chance. I just don't have your strength. I can't be *sure*,
the way you are,' Mari finished miserably.

'But I have to be sure,' he explained awkwardly, the
emotion between them forcing him into a new
honesty. 'I can't bear to doubt. I've *got* to
believe—this time—that fate won't take away the only
person who matters to me. The last two nights, since
you've been in here, I lie awake and want you so
much, and it's a battle to keep from being terrified

that it's going to happen all over again. So I *make* myself believe that this time is different.'

'I'm sorry,' she whispered, forgetting her own pain in the face of his. 'That you should have to go through all this twice—it's not fair.'

'No!' He was suddenly fierce, his embrace almost painful. 'The only unfairness is that you've got to go through this—that you have been going through this for so long. I don't count; my feelings don't matter.'

But they did—more than hers, she realised with a fierceness of her own. He'd been through this kind of thing once before, and had lost Jill. This time—with every fibre of her being—Mari wanted a happy ending for him. This, she supposed, was more of what love was about—this caring more about him than herself, but the insight frightened her as nothing else ever had. To want O'Neil's happy ending meant wanting her own, and wanting anything for herself was tempting fate. Five years ago she had made a deliberate decision to stop wanting or wishing or hoping, and now . . . Well, O'Neil had shattered more than her defences; he had shattered her lofty resolve to isolate herself—and it was painful, she acknowledged bleakly. To care and be cared about created a whole new dimension of pain. And comfort too, she realised, savouring the security of his arms around her and hers around him.

It was too confusing, she concluded wearily, and the confusion—the wild extremes of pain and fierce wanting—haunted her through the next two days, until the final test had been completed.

Then Dr Horner came again to her room, but this time he actually sat down, perching on the end of her bed to regard her with a satisfied smile.

'It looks good, very good,' he announced. 'As I

told you before, you're certainly healthy enough—no problems there. We've got some lovely pictures of your head to study now, and they look very promising to me. Of course the vascular fellows will have to take a look at them, to see if they can spot anything I didn't happen to see, but that's really nothing but a formality. I honestly think it's safe to say that we should be able to go ahead, with every expectation that you'll come out of the surgery very well indeed.'

'As easy as that?' Mari asked awkwardly, afraid to let herself believe. 'I mean—it doesn't seem possible, after what I've been thinking. Are you sure?'

'Of course I'm sure,' Dr Horner answered briskly, stating what was, to him, the obvious. 'I wouldn't say so if I weren't convinced. As far as I'm concerned, it's settled, unless you've changed your mind.'

'No! I want to go ahead with it.' Can he possibly imagine how much I want to go through with it? she asked herself. Can he possibly imagine how much it means to me—how *much* he's given me, given me and O'Neil? 'I haven't changed my mind—believe me!'

'Good. Then it's all over but for the details. You can go home now, by the way,' he added casually, already off her bed and moving towards the door. 'You're officially discharged for the moment, but come back tomorrow—late afternoon. By that time the whole team will have had a chance to review the tests and discuss the case. Come back at—oh, say five, and we'll have you scheduled and ready to go.'

'*Thank you!*' she called after him, and was instantly out of bed. I feel so *free*, she thought, savouring the moment, hugging it to her. I *am* free! I've got a life again. I've got O'Neil, and he and I have got forever now! Lord, just wait until I tell him!

She wanted to do that instantly, but the telephone

seemed too impersonal. She wanted to watch his face when she gave him the news, wanted to see his crooked, devastating smile, wanted to feel his arms around her, wanted everything that he would feel and she would feel again with him.

He would be at work now, she knew. He had been spending each day at his office. 'Not much more than killing time, I'm afraid,' he had told her, 'but it's something to do until I know you're through with each day's testing and I can be with you.' He would surely be at work now; it was only just a little after noon, and there wasn't a reason in the world why she shouldn't go there and tell him the news. After all, Dr Horner had said that she was officially discharged. She would pack up the few things she'd brought with her and O'Neil's mound of gifts, call a cab and—— Look O'Neil Engineering up in the telephone directory first, she reminded herself, thinking how ridiculous it was that she was going to marry the man but had no idea where his offices were located.

O'Neil Engineering was located in one of the older buildings clustered north of the World Trade Center —within reasonable walking distance of where he lived, Mari noted approvingly as she paid the cab driver and crossed the pavement to enter the building. It wasn't until she had intercepted several curious glances that it dawned on her that she hardly fitted in with the others hurrying through the busy lobby or waiting for a lift. Among the crisp and businesslike attire, her hand-embroidered peasant dress was decidedly out of place. To make matters worse, while others were carrying briefcases, she was juggling two plastic bags crammed with her possessions and O'Neil's gifts, and holding the crystal bud vase with its white rose, the only one of O'Neil's floral offerings she hadn't left for the nurses to pass on to other patients.

Given how out of place she looked, she was beginning to think that coming to O'Neil's office hadn't been such a good idea. She was going to stick out like a sore thumb and attract attention, attention he might prefer to avoid. But, before she could change her mind, she was committed, swept into an elevator on a tide of suits and ties, forced to exit a few floors later when the elevator doors opened on to the reception area of O'Neil Engineering.

She hung back while two business types stated their intentions to the efficient young woman at the desk. Finally, when it was Mari's turn, she hesitantly gave her name and asked for O'Neil.

'Of course,' the young woman nodded, carefully masking her curiosity as she gave Mari the once-over. 'Just go along to his office—down that way.'

Nodding her thanks, Mari started down the indicated corridor, only to be met half-way by a plump and motherly woman coming towards her.

'It's Miss Scott, isn't it? Or can I call you Mari? I feel as though I know you that well. Here, let me help you with these,' she offered, not waiting for a reply as she relieved Mari of the bags containing her possessions, leaving her only the bud vase and its single rose. 'I'll bet Gus gave you that,' she observed, leading the way into an office. 'He's been going out of his mind trying to think of things that would please you. I told him I didn't think it mattered, that you'd like anything he brought you, but he wasn't convinced.' She deposited Mari's bags on the one desk in the room, then straightened up to regard Mari with a broad smile. 'So you've been discharged, have you?

Gus didn't think you'd be out this soon. Did the tests go all right?'

'I——' Mari started automatically, then stopped dead, too muddled by this stream of consciousness to know what to say. 'Who's Gus?'

'Who's Gus?' the woman repeated, regarding her with doubtful curiosity now. 'You *are* Mari Scott, aren't you? Gloria said . . .'

'Yes, but . . .' It was Mari's turn to trail off. Gus, she repeated to herself, incredulous. Gus. Angus. An*gus*. 'You call O'Neil *Gus*?'

'Of course. Don't you?'

'No.' Mari shook her head, then added in a strangled voice, 'I call him O'Neil.'

'Oh, well, I suppose he doesn't seem like a Gus to you, any more than you seem like a Marigold to him, although he says he teases you with Marigold sometimes. By the way, I'm Judy Lincoln, Gus's secretary,' the woman explained. 'I've been with him since the start—a kind of older sister then, more like a mother now. Come with me while I try to find him,' she commanded, propelling Mari forward. 'Certainly I've been more like a mother these last few months,' Judy Lincoln continued, picking up on her previous comment as they walked what proved to be a series of narrow corridors and large, well-lit workrooms. 'He didn't know what to make of you, at the start of the summer, and he drove me mad with his wanting to tear off to whatever projects we had going at the ends of the earth, then just as quickly wanting to tear back to Vermont again. The one thing he didn't want to do was stay here in New York and clear off his desk. That's why the last few days have been a godsend. With you in the hospital, he's been keeping his nose pretty close to the grindstone—not that I liked to think that you were facing something quite so serious.'

'He told you about it?' Mari managed to get in.

'He tells me pretty nearly everything, and always has,' Mrs Lincoln conceded complacently. 'Only in his weak moments, though, and there've been a lot of those this summer, I can tell you! There are times when I've wondered how much more the poor man can take. After Jill and that terrible year . . . Well, he never expected to find anyone else—didn't *want* to find anyone else. "That's over for me, Judy," he said more than once, and he meant it too—until he met you. And then he fought so hard against you, which didn't work, of course. And just when he'd accepted the inevitable and knew what he wanted to do . . . It was a bit of a facer, to find that he was going to have to deal with something that cuts quite so close to the bone.'

'I know. That's why——'

'—you tried to end things between you,' Mrs Lincoln finished for her, 'but thank heavens you didn't. He needs to have things turn out right this time. If any man needs that, Gus does, and I suppose there's a chance? You must know something by now, but I expect you'd rather tell him first.'

'Well, yes . . .'

'And so you shall.' It didn't surprise Mari in the least when Mrs Lincoln actually patted her hand. 'If we can find him, that is. The man's never where you want him. I thought he might be in here,' she explained, stopping in the middle of yet another workroom, hopefully surveying the ranks of drawing-boards with men and women bent over them. 'Anyone seen Gus?' she called out.

'In the conference-room, I think,' one of the women

offered, briefly glancing up from her work. 'At least, that's where he said he was going.'

'Worth a try.' Mrs Lincoln was off again, urging Mari forward. 'I hope you'll be gentle with him,' she cautioned as they approached the door at the end of the corridor. 'He's vulnerable—far more so than anyone knows. He——Yes, here he is,' she added unnecessarily when she had the door open.

It was an O'Neil Mari had never seen before, one she had never even imagined. He had obviously started the day in a business suit, but somewhere along the line had shed the jacket, loosened his tie and rolled up his sleeves. Now, with one hand braced against the edge of a table, he stood with three other men, poring over a set of plans. In his other hand, one of his thin cigars burned unnoticed, serving as a kind of pointer as he gestured towards one section of the plans.

'I don't see how you can think this will work,' he was saying, very much in control. 'The underpinnings are wrong. It's going to take the stress here and here.' He indicated two points on the drawing, then a third. 'They won't hold, gentlemen.' He bent further across the table, his hand extended as he traced a line. 'You see, there——It's Mari!' he breathed as something—some movement of hers, perhaps—made him look up. He stared at her for a long moment, his face a cautious mask, his gaze locked on hers while the cigar fell unnoticed from his grasp to begin to scorch a small area of the drawings beneath his hand. 'Good lord,' he managed. 'You should have called! Is everything—is something wrong?'

'Nothing's wrong,' she told him, the world contracting, drawing it on itself to shut out Mrs Lincoln beside her, the three men ranged around him. 'Nothing's wrong at all. In fact, things couldn't be more right, O'Neil.'

'Thank goodness!' He was around the table instantly, his loose-limbed marionette's figure closing the distance between them. Deftly, in the moment before he drew her into his arms and she slipped hers around his neck, Mrs Lincoln took the crystal bud vase from her unresisting fingers.

'Thank goodness,' O'Neil said again, his lips against her hair, and Mari heard her own voice, as unsteady as his had been, telling him,

'It's going to be all right, O'Neil. Dr Horner says we can have forever.'

CHAPTER EIGHT

'TELL me more,' O'Neil commanded when they had left the office and the building behind to find themselves some privacy on the crowded street. 'Tell me everything he said.'

Mari did, while they walked slowly, thoughtfully, his arm around her shoulders and hers around his waist, holding close against the jostling of business people. She found that what Dr Horner had told her—his *gift*!—had so impressed itself upon her mind that she could repeat almost his exact words to O'Neil.

'That's all?' he asked when she was done.

'Isn't that enough?' She stopped and turned to face him, oblivious to the flow of pedestrians breaking around them. 'After all, it's what you've been telling me from the start—I've got a chance. It's practically a guarantee!'

'I don't believe in guarantees.'

'I didn't either, not until Dr Horner talked to me. Perhaps, if you'd heard him—heard how confident he sounded . . .'

'Perhaps.'

Perhaps, Mari repeated to herself as O'Neil's arm came around her shoulders once more and they walked on. I tell him this—this incredible news—and all he can say is, 'Perhaps'! 'You don't sound terribly happy about it,' she ventured.

'Lord, it's got nothing to do with whether I'm happy about it! It's just that it's hard to absorb—

hard to believe—after all the black thoughts I've been thinking these last few days. It almost seems too good to be true—too easy.'

'I think we're entitled to something easy for a change,' she countered. 'Heaven knows, after what happened to you—with Jill—you're *due* something easy!'

'And you're not, I suppose?' he asked with bitter irony. 'The five years of quiet hell you've put in don't count?'

'Not as much. It's not as though I'd lost anything.'

'Only your future.'

'But that wasn't real. It wasn't something I possessed, a known quantity of happiness that got torn away from me. If anything, my life got better because of what I was told.'

'Mari,' he asked with ominous calm, 'are you always this noble?'

'But it's true! I put my life in order, started doing only what I wanted to do—what *pleased* me. I——' She stopped and then smiled up at him. 'O'Neil, do you realise what we're doing?'

'Arguing about which of us had it harder?'

'No. We're behaving like people in love, I think. I never realised it was quite this clear-cut—this business of caring more about the other person. The worst of it is that once you start doing that, and the other person is caring about you, you've got to let yourself be cared about. It's confusing, and not as easy as I thought.'

'But we are learning,' he told her, returning her smile. 'It may be hard, and confusing, but we are.'

'Yes.' Again she felt that same sense of being *free*—free to love, free to be happy, she decided, moving even closer to him as they walked on in a silence of contentment.

Having skirted the towering complex of the World Trade Center, they passed the quiet charm of Trinity Church and its graveyard, finally leaving the shadowed canyons of the streets to enter the green and sunlit space of Battery Park. Ahead, even on a weekday afternoon, large crowds were waiting for the ferry out to the Statue of Liberty which stood sentinel in the harbour.

'Is it unpatriotic to admit that I've never been out there?' Mari asked as they stood watching the colourful scene.

'If it is, I'm as guilty as you.'

'Two typical New Yorkers!' she laughed, savouring the sunshine and the moment. 'We're terrible!'

'Do you want to do it now? We can, if you like.'

'No. Not today, in a crowd like that,' she decided. 'We'll wait until some cold day in January, when no one else wants to go.'

'All right,' O'Neil agreed easily enough, but unspoken between them was the fact that something significant had happened. Some day in January—some day in the future—would do for the Statue. They had dared to save the Statue for another day.

They took one of the walks to the left, away from the crowds, passing all the street vendors with their counterfeit designer watches. 'I suppose you've already got a Rolex,' Mari teased.

'Why?' O'Neil grinned down at her. 'Were you planning to buy me one?'

'Mmm, maybe. I expect I could afford it here.' Then she stopped dead when she saw the hot-dog cart ahead. 'I *will* buy you one of those,' she promised, urging him forward. 'I could kill for one right now—with everything on it.'

Ignoring his protests, she bought two, handing one

to him when they found an empty bench and sat down close together. 'Lord, there's nothing like this in Vermont,' she said through her first bite. 'I've missed these!'

'You've missed more than these,' O'Neil observed, watching her with an abstracted smile. 'When we're walking, I see the way you devour things with your eyes. I think you've missed the whole city.'

'Yes, but——'

'You're not actually going to say it, are you?' He groaned, then said it for her. 'It's a nice place to visit, but you wouldn't want to live here.'

'Well, it's true,' she countered indignantly. 'A little of New York goes a long way, and I *like* Vermont better! I'm happier there.'

'I'm not arguing with your sentiments, love. It's just the cliché I object to. What you want is the best of both worlds.'

'Cliché,' she mumbled through a mouthful of hot dog and sauerkraut.

'I know. I'm no better than you are,' he admitted cheerfully, finally biting into his own hot dog, chewing reflectively. 'You know,' he resumed, 'we want the same things, you and I—small doses of the city, when we want challenge or excitement, but a safe harbour—a home—in those quiet green hills.'

'They're mountains.'

'Not very tall ones—and don't be contentious, Marigold Scott. What I'm trying to say is that when we're married, we'll live in Vermont. We can keep the place here, and come back whenever we please, but Vermont will be home. There's no need for me to keep working as hard as I have been. I don't *need* the work any longer—no more empty hours to fill—and there are people to take over much of what I've been doing, while I manage the rest from a distance. After so many years, and thanks to you, I want to be settled. Besides, Vermont's a good place—better than here, certainly—to raise our children.'

Our children. The words struck Mari with a piercing sweetness. Our children. O'Neil's and mine. Was it really possible? He had mentioned children before, but that had been before being told her problem could be corrected; O'Neil had been whistling in the dark then, and they had both known it. And Dr Horner had mentioned children too, Mari reflected, but it had been easy for him to do when he wasn't directly involved. This time was different; O'Neil *meant* what he said—just as she had meant what she said when she had decided to visit the Statue of Liberty in January. Both were promises and the courage to believe in the future, but *children*? Children were different, incredibly real, the reality of love and marriage. *Was* all that possible? Or had O'Neil finally pushed their dreams too far, tempted fate beyond its limits?

Suddenly Mari's demons were back, this time with such a terrible vengeance that she wondered how she could have forgotten them even for a minute. The demons would make her pay—make O'Neil pay too—for daring to believe there was a future for her. Something would happen, things would go wrong. Somehow, in the end, the demons would have their way, but not as she had always thought they would. She had thought it was her life they wanted, but she had been wrong. Her life was now so woven into O'Neil's that it had no meaning of its own. Taking her life now was immaterial, and the demons knew that; they were after the bigger prize. It was love the demons wanted to destroy, the love she and O'Neil had managed to build between them—and all for nothing, she thought with sick despair.

'Mari?' O'Neil prompted gently, breaking through her black thoughts. 'How does that sound? Is it all right with you?'

Is it all right? How could she answer him? What could she say? How could she say anything while the demons danced in her head. *No*! she told herself with savage, primitive fury. She would not—could not—let the demons win! Not now, not when everything she wanted for her life was here and now.

With an intensity that left her shaken, she forced herself to turn towards O'Neil, forced herself to focus her whole being on his face, his love, his strength. 'Of course that's all right with me.' She barely heard her voice; it sounded far away and faint, so she forced herself to speak again. 'It's more than all right, O'Neil.' Her voice was louder now, and that gave her courage. 'I couldn't ask for more.'

When she saw his slow smile, she knew she had won. I've won, she told the demons as O'Neil drew her close. I've won, I've won, I've won, she chanted like a mantra. The words repeated themselves endlessly for all the time they sat in silence and sunshine, holding each other close.

'My feet hurt,' she complained, kicking off her shoes the moment O'Neil let them into his house. 'I'd forgotten how hard concrete is, and I think I'm out of condition after four days in the hospital.'

'Perhaps you did too much,' O'Neil suggested, watching as she moved lightly around the room, renewing her brief acquaintaince with it. 'I shouldn't have kept you out so long, or made you walk so far.'

'Oh, no.' She turned to come back to where he still stood, just inside the door. 'I loved every minute of it.

Still, it's good to be home.' Impulsively, she went up on her toes, stretching to link her arms around his neck. 'This still will be home when we're in New York, won't it?'

'If you like.'

'Oh, I do. It's like you—unexpected and comfortable and attractive—in spite of the fact that all the bare bones of the engineering show. At least there's no pre-stressed concrete,' she added, waiting for him to smile. When he didn't, she studied his face and then asked, 'What's wrong, O'Neil?'

'I suppose I'm worrying about you. Do you think you should rest for a while?'

'No, but I'd kill for a bath right now. I'd forgotten that the city's dirty too,' she explained. 'All of me feels slightly grimy. And don't worry about me, O'Neil. I'm no different from what I was before you knew there was anything to worry about.' She stretched further, touching her lips to his cheek, then started for the stairs. 'I won't be long,' she promised from the first landing, 'and then we'll think about supper.'

Something had happened to him, Mari mused while she soaked in the depths of his absurd Victorian tub. At some point during their long walk home, he'd changed from the way he had been when they were sitting on the bench in Battery Park, holding each other close. Just now, downstairs, there had been a hard edge about him, a stiffness in the way he'd been holding himself, a shading of caution in his eyes.

It wasn't fair, she decided, leaning back into the curve of the tub and closing her eyes. Just as she'd managed to banish her demons for good, O'Neil's had come back. Or perhaps they had never left, and all that fine talk about marriage and children and where they would live had been nothing more than an attempt to keep them at bay.

And what could she do? she wondered, her thoughts begining to drift. There had to be some way to reach him, to make him believe. All along, he had been her strength and her courage; now it seemed it was her turn to give strength and courage to him, if she could only think of a way . . .

The cooling water finally recalled her to the present and drove her out of the tub to dry herself. When she was done, she wrapped the enormous towel around herself, toga fashion, and opened the bathroom door.

Through the wall of windows, the slanting rays of the last of the sun momentarily blinded her, and she had collided with O'Neil before she realised he was there. Instantly she felt his hands gripping her arms, heard him urgently ask, 'Mari, what's wrong? You were in there so long. Love, what's happened?'

She shook her head, trying to get her bearings. 'Nothing.'

'But you just stumbled.'

'Over you, idiot.' Her eyes had adjusted to the light now, but that didn't help much. O'Neil was impossible to read, standing with his back to the windows, his face deeply shadowed. 'Look, you've got to stop worrying about me! I'm not fragile. I'm not going to break, so why now—just when the news is as good as it possibly could be—do you have to start hovering?'

'I don't know.' Abruptly he released her and went to stand by the windows, hands driven deep into his pockets.

'It doesn't make any sense,' she told him, climbing on to his bed, carefully realigning the edges of the towel to preserve her modesty. 'All along you've been the one convinced that something could be done. I thought you were crazy. *I* was the one with the doubts, but now—when you've been proved right—you're the one with the doubts and I'm not. So what happened, O'Neil?'

'Who knows? Maybe it's that it sounds too good to be true, or the fear that I've dragged you into something dangerous. If happy endings don't happen to me, what right do I have to involve you in my bad luck?'

'It's hardly your bad luck that I was born with this thing wrong in my head.'

'No, I know that. That's not what I mean. It's that perhaps it might be better for you if I weren't involved. If you must have the surgery, it might be safer if you weren't—this sounds mad!—under the cloud of my bad luck, I suppose.'

'What do you mean?' she asked carefully, striving for cool logic. 'If I'd gone to Dr Horner all by myself, things would be different? He'd do the surgery and everything would be fine, but just because we're together, it won't?'

'Something like that,' he admitted awkwardly. 'I told you it sounded mad.'

'Or just plain dumb,' she contributed. 'I don't believe you're saying it, much less thinking it. It's the sort of thing I'd expect *me* to think! You're the cool and logical engineer, and you've suddenly gone all superstitious on me.'

'I know. It doesn't make much sense, does it?'

'None. I'm going to have the surgery, and whatever is going to happen will happen—no matter whether I'm with you or not.'

'Yes. The surgery.' He turned away from the windows and came to sit on the edge of the bed, looking at her. 'Perhaps that's the problem—that the surgery is real at last. Mari, am I asking too much of you? Am I forcing you into something you'd rather not face?'

'I thought so once,' she answered honestly, 'but not any more.' She reached for his hand, lacing her fingers through his. 'O'Neil, you didn't force me into this. No one can force me into something I don't want to do, but I *want* to do this! It's true that I wouldn't have wanted to—wouldn't even have known the possibility existed—if it hadn't been for you, if I hadn't met you. Until then I was quite content to accept what I thought was my fate, to have what I could for as long as I could, and then let it go. But it's too late for that now. You're too much to let go, and I won't let you go—at least, not without a fight.

'Don't worry, O'Neil,' she continued quickly when his sombre expression didn't change. She leaned forward, closing the distance between them, touching her hand to his face. 'I don't know what else I can say, except that I really believe everything's going to be all right.'

'I don't know how you can say that.'

'Because we're together. O'Neil, I learned one thing after five years of being the noble stoic, all alone with this thing.'

'What's that?' he asked with the ghost of a smile.

'I learned that it's better not to be alone, that things began to go better the moment I let you into my life and *wasn't* alone any more. And if things have gone so much better so far, why should my luck stop now?

'Why indeed?'

He wanted to be convinced; through the touch of the palm of her hand on his cheek, she could feel him fighting to be convinced, but it wasn't quite working.

There's something more! she thought. I've got to do something more . . . and in that moment the answer came so quickly to her that it left her shaken, suddenly breathless. 'O'Neil, kiss me.'

'Do you think that's wise?'

'Absolutely.' She rose up on her knees, linking her arms around his neck. 'Please.'

'How can I refuse?' he asked, and this time he really did smile just before his lips captured hers.

They were—both of them—hungry, she realised as their kiss deepened. They were hungry for something more substantial that words, and what Mari had thought she was doing only for him she now realised she was doing just as much for herself. She too needed this kind of closeness, this kind of being together; all the things she had only been able to imagine before were suddenly real, and she just as suddenly needed them all.

'Mari, we're playing with fire,' O'Neil said unsteadily, ending their kiss. 'We could get carried away.'

'Good.' She sat back on her heels in order to see him properly. 'That's what we need, I think—no more doubts, no more worries. We need each other, O'Neil. We need to get carried away.'

'But not now,' he countered. 'In the circumstances —Mari, for heaven's sake! Your towel is coming loose.'

'Good.' Of course she had known it was; it was precisely what she had hoped would happen at this point, and the fact that things were going according to plan gave her the courage to be even bolder. 'And the circumstances be damned,' she added, methodically beginning to unbutton his shirt.

'Mari, what the hell are you doing?'

'Right now, I'm afraid I'm seducing you.' As she got the last button free, the end of the towel slipped until only the swell of her breasts was holding it in place. Perfect! she told herself, pulling his shirt loose from his trousers, spreading it open. She placed her hands on his chest, fingers spread, her palms against his hard flesh. 'A long time ago, you said I'd have to seduce you, and I seem to be succeeding,' she noted when she heard his quick intake of breath, felt the rapid beat of his heart.

'You know you are, and I know damn well what you're trying to do for me.'

'No, O'Neil, I'm not doing it for you,' she whispered, leaning closer, touching his lips with the tip of her tongue, teasing lightly, destroying the last of his control. 'I'm doing this for both of us.'

With a smothered groan, his mouth closed on hers, his arms came around her, holding her to him while he kissed her with a wild thoroughness—possessing her, drawing her into him, joining them in a way they had never been joined before. Together, they fell back against the pillows, lying side by side while he worked the towel away and she fumbled with the buckle of his belt.

'Witch,' he murmured raggedly when his lips finally left hers to find the pulse beating at the base of her throat and then moved lower, tracing the curve of her breast. 'Do you know what you're doing to me?'

Surely not as much as he was doing to her, she told herself, uttering a little cry and arching towards him as his mouth continued its clever explorations. Vaguely, she grasped the fact that she had lost control; the balance had shifted and he was the aggressor now. But that wasn't the proper term, she decided in the moment before her thoughts went spinning away.

O'Neil didn't need to be the aggressor; instead, he was enchanting her, murmuring words of love, using his lips and his hands to find a hundred—no, a thousand—ways to please her . . . a thousand ways to make her ache for more.

The need for him consumed her; it was a mindless wanting. His touch was an exquisite torment, driving her to new and unimagined heights while she stirred beneath him. Feverishly her hands slid across the hard-bunched muscles of his shoulders and his back, trying to draw him closer, trying to reach the final moment of release.

And when it came—that infinity of union and completion—it was deeper, richer, greater . . . beyond all comprehension. Mari heard her own soft, breathless cry, felt his last shuddering tremor, and then the frenzy began to ebb away, leaving in its wake a kind of closeness and contentment unlike anything she had ever known before.

'Thank you, O'Neil,' she whispered, reaching up to touch his face. 'That was everything.'

'And more, my love,' he murmured, keeping her close when he turned on his side, pillowing her head on his shoulder. 'So much more.'

And even more than that, she realised, her last coherent thought before she slept.

Once, and then again, they awoke during the dark hours of the night, coming together each time with a new awareness and familiarity. Now their explorations were leisurely, even languid, as they savoured the dazzling sensations of taste and touch. In the darkness, Mari learned to give in return, her tentative caresses growing bolder as O'Neil responded to her touch.

'You told me this,' she whispered once, bending

over him, her hands kneading at his shoulders while her lips teased with his, 'and you were absolutely right.'

'Right about what?' he asked lazily, and in the darkness she could hear his smile. 'What did I say?'

'That when we finally made love, and it was as good as you knew it would be, I'd wonder why I hadn't been willing to do it sooner.' She paused to explore the breadth of his shoulders and the hard muscles of his chest, feeling his breathing begin to quicken beneath her touch. 'Is it as good as you thought it would be?'

'You know it is, my love,' he murmured, his voice slurring slightly, roughened by desire. 'Better than good. Better than I could have imagined.'

'You said I'd feel like an idiot to have waited, and we agreed that you'd say, "I told you so",' she continued, her hands drifting lower, caressing the flat planes of his stomach. 'Now's your chance, O'Neil.'

'Lord, I can't,' he told her on a long, unsteady breath, his hands tangling in her hair to draw her mouth to his. 'Can't think . . . Mari love, you're driving me mad!'

'Good,' she breathed, finally relenting to meet his lips, the possession of his kiss shattering her own control.

This must be heaven, she thought—this wanting, this kind of closeness, this sharing, this overwhelming, all-consuming love. Everything she had ever wanted was here in O'Neil's embrace, in giving him pleasure, in giving herself completely to his need and her own.

And in the morning, when she awoke, she found another kind of heaven. She lay lazy and contented within the circle of his arm, listening to the deep, slow regularity of his breathing. He was still asleep, and cautiously she raised herself up on one elbow to study his face.

She had never seen him like this, never watched his face when he had no awareness of her. She had never seen his face absent of all emotion except for the perhaps imagined smile she hoped she was seeing now. Asleep, he seemed younger; the creases by his mouth and the network at the corners of his eyes were smoothed out and fainter now. Thick hair slanted untidily, almost boyishly across his forehead, its rich darkness repeated in his long lashes. In the soft light of morning, the clean, sharp edge of his profile was softened, dark stubble blurring the thrusting outline of his chin.

As though sensing the intensity of her gaze, he stirred but did not wake. He turned a little more towards her, his free arm disturbing the sheet when he reached out for her, his hand settling possessively on the soft curve of her hip. Instinctively, her gaze was drawn to the angular lines of his body; she found herself absorbed completely by the length of hair-roughened thigh, lean flank and narrow waist. All this she had explored and learned in last night's darkness, she realised with a sudden stir of emotion. He was all so known to her now, belonging to her in the same way every inch of her now belonged to him.

'You're awake before me,' she heard him say, and turned to see his lazy smile, his eyes deep blue and narrowed slightly against the morning light. 'Are you happy, love?'

'You know I am.' She bent to kiss him briefly, her hair a tangled cloud around her face. 'And you?'

'Absolutely,' he answered, stretching like a large, dangerously graceful but contented cat. 'Whatever it was—that superstitious nonsense and my doubts——'

'Your demons,' Mari supplied, resting her head again on the pillow of his shoulder.

'Is that what they were?' O'Neil thought a moment. 'Yes, that's what they were, but you drove them away—with a vengeance, Marigold Scott.'

'I told you never to call me that,' she protested, pretending to pull away. 'I keep telling you and you keep doing it. If you don't stop, I'll start calling you Gus.'

'Everyone else does,' he told her with such deceptive calmness that she missed the careful, watchful expression in his eyes. 'Why shouldn't you?'

'Because you don't seem like a Gus to me. I don't think I could fall in love with a Gus. I might have one as a friend, but I wouldn't fall in love with him. Heavens, O'Neil, I had enough trouble falling in love with Angus O'Neil—which is what you told me your name was that first morning. You never mentioned that people call you Gus, and I was busy fighting the battle of Angus.'

'What's wrong with Angus?'

'What's wrong is that Nate has a Black Angus bull, and as long as I thought of you as Angus, you were going to be some kind of macho super-stud! That's why I settled on O'Neil. It didn't offend my feminist sensibilities.'

'Ah!' He expelled a long breath, then pulled her down upon him, laughter rumbling in his chest. 'And all this time I thought O'Neil was a way to keep me at a distance.'

'O'Neil was a way of letting you get close.'

'Which you are now,' he noted, holding her in place, her lips just inches from his own.

'So I am,' she whispered, her heart already beating faster as the friction of his body against hers began to work its spell. 'What are you going to do about that, O'Neil?'

'Nothing, at the moment. I'm starving!'

'Mmm, so am I.'

'But for food, this time,' he told her firmly. 'What do you say to dim sum?'

'You're serious, aren't you?'

'Absolutely,' he assured her with a grin. 'What you've got in mind will have to wait, my love.'

'All right.' She gave in with good grace, permitting him to release her. 'Come to think of it, we never did have supper, and it's been years since I've had dim sum for breakfast. In fact, the more I think about it,' she told him, answering his grin, 'the more I think I'd kill for dim sum right now. And why do I keep saying that?' she wondered aloud. 'I never have before.'

'You're saying it now because you've stopped being the noble stoic, grimly accepting fate without a murmur. You've started believing you can have what you want.'

'And what I want most is you, O'Neil!'

'But breakfast first,' he countered firmly. 'It's time you learned how much better making love is after a brief bout of self-denial.'

He had been right about that, Mari discovered later, after the enormous meal they had shared in the nondescript Chinese restaurant in the Bowery that had always been her favourite. This time, making love in O'Neil's huge Victorian bed, they had done their best to prolong the moment—trying to hold it all in memory, she decided while she was still capable of coherent thought. They were facing—possibly even

today—the beginning of a longer ordeal of separation
and this time their pleasure wasn't only for the
moment. This time the memory of sensation and
emotion would have to see them through the empty
days ahead.

'This time may have to last a while,' O'Neil said
later, speaking her thoughts aloud when the moment
was finally past and they lay together in contented
satisfaction. 'It may be a while before we can do this
again.'

'I know.' She nodded, feeling a stirring of
unease—for him, not for herself. 'O'Neil? Are you
sure you're going to be all right? That this time isn't
going to be too much like—like the last?'

'Like Jill, you mean?' he supplied calmly enough,
but she had felt the sudden tension in him, could feel
it grow as he continued, 'But this time isn't going to
be the same. This time, something *can* be done. I
won't have to stand by, helpless, watching. Lord, all
those months of watching! I can stand anything but
that, and each day you'll be getting better—there's the
difference. Besides, he told her, linking his hand with
hers, 'you're the one we should be thinking of—not
me.'

'No, it's both of us,' she corrected firmly. 'We're in
this together, Angus O'Neil!'

CHAPTER NINE

'I'M afraid this isn't going to be as simple as I thought.' Today, Dr Horner had chosen to seat himself behind his desk, and now he faced Mari and O'Neil across its untidy expanse. 'Yesterday, when I spoke to you, all the test results looked good, and I saw no reason why this shouldn't be a straightforward corrective procedure. Unfortunately, when the vascular men got their first look at the pictures, they spotted something I hadn't seen.'

'Which was?' O'Neil prompted impatiently while Mari sat beside him, unable to speak, a terrible chill stealing over her.

'There's a second malformation,' Dr Horner explained, opening Mari's file and staring down at the scribbled notes on the first page. 'It's a smaller one, to be sure—so small, in fact, that it was almost overlooked. It's in a smaller vessel, one behind the problem vessel we already knew about.'

'And what about it?' probed O'Neil, leaning forward in his chair. 'Is it trouble?'

'Unfortunately, yes.'

'But if it's smaller,' Mari put in, finding her voice, 'and in a smaller vessel, how can it be trouble?'

'Because it's in a more critical part of the brain,' Dr Horner told her, his face a careful mask. 'Technically, it can be corrected, but it won't be easy to reach, and it won't be easy to work on.'

'And what does that mean for Mari?' O'Neil demanded, tension in his voice for the first time.

'It means that there's a higher probability of permanent damage being done during the surgery. This vessel is much deeper and getting to it will be difficult, so the potential for damage to other parts of the brain is far greater. Even if the surgery is successful—if I'm able to reach the vessel and repair it without any problem—I can't guarantee that Mari won't be left with some permanent disability.'

'What kind of disability?' Mari managed to ask.

'Anything, from a slight weakness in your left arm and leg to total paralysis of the left side of your body. I'm sorry I can't be more precise than that, but there are just too many unknowns.'

'And if the surgery isn't successful?' O'Neil was the first to find the courage to ask the question uppermost in both their minds. 'What happens then?'

'She won't die—that much I can tell you,' Dr Horner offered quickly. 'With my team, in the controlled conditions of the operating-room, we'll be able to handle any problem quickly enough to keep her alive.'

'. . . keep her alive.' The words echoed wildly in Mari's head, and she didn't need to ask what they meant. She already knew—and so did O'Neil, she realised when she turned to look at him. His face was grey beneath his tan, his features set and rigid.

'But I'd never regain consciousness,' she said flatly, aware of O'Neil's quickly checked movement, as though he had wanted to keep her from saying the words. 'Isn't that right?'

'Yes, I'm afraid so.' For an instant, Dr Horner's gaze flickered away from hers, and then returned. 'This doesn't mean that any of these things *will* happen. There's a possibility that the surgery will be completely successful. It's a slim possibility, to be sure, but it does exist. It's ironic that the problem that brought you here in the first place is—relatively speaking—no problem at all. If that were the only repair needed, I'd be feeling very optimistic now.

'But in the circumstances,' he continued after a pause, 'I can't be optimistic, and it wouldn't be fair to you if I misrepresented the problem.'

'No, of course not,' Mari agreed, painfully aware of O'Neil's rigid silence, knowing that—for the moment, at least—she had to be strong for both of them. 'So now the only question is for me to decide if I want to take the chance and have the surgery.'

'I suppose that's one way of looking at it,' Dr Horner agreed uncomfortably, 'although I don't really see that you've got any choice. As poor as your chances may be, as damaging as the surgery can be, it at least gives you some chance. Doing nothing gives you none at all. Either one of these malformations will kill you within a reasonably short period of time.'

'By the time I'm thirty,' Mari supplied with bitterness. 'Isn't that about right?'

'You might have longer. Perhaps as much as another five years, given the healthy life you lead. You'll have to decide if a possible five years means more to you than the admittedly slight chance of successful surgery and a normal life expectancy. The surgery might give you that.'

'Or it might give me nothing at all.'

'Mari, no!' O'Neil broke his silence at last, turning towards her and putting out his hand in mute appeal. 'For pity's sake, don't say that!'

Why not? she wanted to scream. What difference does it make what I say or do? We're trapped, O'Neil, both of us, and nothing I say or do is going to change it! The demons have well and truly caught up with both of us, and this time there's *no* way out, *no* chance of a happy ending.

'Well, thank you, Dr Horner,' she said, her voice surprisingly composed. 'I'll need some time to think this through, but I'll let you know—either way—as soon as I've made my decision.' Not that there was any decision to be made, she reflected as she and O'Neil stood up to leave the office. Her decision had been made years ago; the only thing now was to convince O'Neil of its rightness.

The reaction didn't begin to set in until they were out on the street. Then, amid the height of rush-hour confusion, buffeted by passers-by and assaulted by the harsh sounds of traffic, Mari began to tremble, and then to shake. Instantly O'Neil's arms were around her, drawing her into the shelter and protection of his embrace.

She never knew how long the two of them stood there like that, but at last, when the worst of the attack had passed, she managed to say, 'I want to go home—back to Vermont.'

'Of course. Just give me time to arrange for the plane. We can leave within a couple of hours.'

'No, I want to go now. Alone.'

'Mari, I'm not going to let you go alone. You can't be alone now.'

'But I've got to be! Don't you see, O'Neil? We don't have any choice.'

'Of course we do, but you're not thinking clearly right now. We'll go home—back to my place—and give you a little time to pull yourself together. Then we can decide what to do.'

'I've already decided!'

But he wasn't having any part of her objections. He ignored them to hurry her towards the waiting car, not speaking during the long trip downtown, through congested streets, to his house. Once inside, he immediately poured each of them a stiff measure of brandy. 'Here, drink up,' he commanded, handing one glass to her. 'We both need this.'

Huddled in the corner of one of the leather couches, Mari obediently sipped and began to feel a little warmth breaking through the icy cold enveloping her. At the same time, she began to think a little more clearly, began to realise that her first instinct to flee wouldn't do. She would have to be logical now, have to find some clearly logical way to make O'Neil understand.

'Mari.' He disarmed her by taking the initiative, drawing a chair close to where she sat, leaning forward until his gaze could connect with hers. 'I never dreamed it would come to this, never dreamed I'd force you into such a difficult situation.'

'It's an impossible situation——' she began, but he cut her off.

'No, hear me out before you say anything. I just want you to understand that I'll accept your decision—whatever it is. If the surgery is what you want, we'll face it together. If it's not, then at least we'll have those five years Dr Horner talked about. The important thing is that you do what's right for you.'

For a moment there, she had thought it was going to be easy. If only he had stopped after the bit about accepting her decision, it would have been easy. The problem was that he'd continued to speak, which meant that his thoughts had also gone further. He was talking about five years together when there could be no question of that. She took another sip of brandy—for courage—and began to speak.

'I do know what I'm going to do,' she told him, and watched as his eyes closed briefly, a reflex action against what he thought were two equally unthinkable alternatives. 'I'm not going to have the surgery. I don't even want to think about the possible outcome Dr Horner described. Instead, I'm going back to Vermont. Alone.'

'For how long?'

'Forever. For as long as I have.' This was the hard part, she realised, fighting the first stirrings of panic. It wasn't going to be easy for her, but by the sudden stubborn set of his features, she knew O'Neil was going to make it more difficult still. 'We can't see each other again, O'Neil. It's got to be over now.'

'No! For heaven's sake, Mari, there's no need for that! At least let us share whatever time you have.'

'That won't work.'

'Why not?'

'Because we'd both be miserable. This would tear us apart, and I'd rather have been happy for a little while than miserable for the next five years.'

'It won't be like that!'

'It would,' she insisted. 'We'd spend the next five years counting days, wondering if it really would be five years, wondering if it would be more or less.'

'It wouldn't——'

'It *would*!' she cried. 'I know, O'Neil. I've already spent nearly five years that way and I know what it's like. It's bad enough to do it alone; I couldn't do it with someone watching me all the time.'

'We'd be together.'

'No, we wouldn't. This thing would be between us—always—and as time passed, it would only get worse. I've done it, and it's an incredibly passive kind of thing, and you're not a passive person. Sooner or later, you'd decide that even the risks of surgery were better than how we were living.'

'No, I wouldn't—not unless it was what you wanted to do.'

'But you would,' she corrected gently. 'Do you think, during the last five years, that I haven't wanted to find a quick fix? Up until the day I met you, if someone had offered me the possibility of an operation, even one with such poor odds as now, I'd have taken it in a minute!'

'Then why not take it now?'

'Because everything has changed,' she countered stubbornly. 'Now I'm afraid of the surgery. If we were living together——'

'If we were married, you mean.'

'Whatever. All the time we were together, I'd be afraid. I'd be a coward, and always confused, fighting not to do what you wanted me to. No, O'Neil, it just wouldn't work!'

'It would.'

'It *wouldn't*!' Suddenly she couldn't bear it—couldn't bear to have O'Neil so close, couldn't bear the way he was looking at her, his own anguish clear, couldn't bear the way he was caring. She got up, carefully skirting his chair. Wrapping her arms tightly around herself to try to contain the pain, she began to pace. 'You're not being fair. All I want to do is go back to Vermont and try to be empty again. The only way I know how to handle something like this is to be empty—not to care—and you're trying to take that away from me,' she cried, her voice beginning to waver. 'It's the only thing I've got left, and you won't let me have it!'

'Mari, my love, I don't want to make you unhappy——'

'You don't want to make me unhappy?' she shrilled, turning on him. 'What in heaven's name do you think I am? I've been unhappy since the instant Dr Horner began to talk. Don't be so damned self-important, O'Neil! You didn't make me unhappy; all you're doing is making it worse.'

Lord, she thought, going to stand by the windows, leaning her head against the cool glass, it was going to be worse than she thought. No matter what she said, he didn't want to take no for an answer, wasn't going to take no for an answer unless she could find some way to convince him, some way without telling him the whole of her reasons.

'Please, O'Neil. You said you'd accept my decision; why won't you do it? I know it's not *your* decision, but why should that make any difference?'

'Because it doesn't make any sense.' Suddenly he was behind her, his arms around her, holding her close. 'There's so much between us—you know it! We're in love in a way that doesn't happen very often, and you're trying to leave us with nothing. You won't give us five years; you won't give us a chance at forever. I *can't* accept a decision like that!'

He would have to, she knew, but his embrace had momentarily breached her defences. She knew she ought to pull away, take up the battle again—and she would—but not just yet . . .

In the long run, she had no choice. When he talked about five years together, he couldn't know what he was asking of her. Just the impossible; it was as simple as that. She couldn't handle five years with him; she wanted forever, *needed* forever . . . and the crumb of five years would be five years of hell. If it hadn't been for what he had endured with Jill, she would have taken the chance for forever, taken it in a moment. But there had been Jill; that nightmare year at her bedside had happened for him, and Mari couldn't let that happen to him again.

She couldn't run the risk of being *kept* alive! At all costs, she had to avoid that possibility. It was the one thing she couldn't do to O'Neil; neither could she explain it to him. He would be noble and brave and tell her not to worry about him, to go ahead and have the surgery. He would forget all about what he'd told her just a few hours before—'All those months of watching. I can stand anything but that,' he had said, and she loved him too much to ask that of him. She couldn't put him into a situation where he might have to do exactly that.

'No, this way was better, better for both of them and certainly better for him. End it now—a clean break—and there wouldn't be those months of watching for him. In time, he would begin to forget her; he might not be happy again, he would become as detached and restless as he'd been before, but at least he knew *how* to find some accommodation with being alone. He knew as much about being alone as she knew about living with a time limit. Apart, they wouldn't be happy, but at least they'd manage, and for neither of them would there be the hell that being together would bring. No, in every way this was better—the *only* solution—or would be when it stopped hurting so much.

'O'Neil, it won't work,' she said at last, breaking the long silence between them. 'Perhaps it would work for you, but I couldn't bear it.' That's it, Mari, a detached part of her mind was telling her. Appeal to his nobility or his sense of fair play. 'If you love me as much as you say you do, you'll accept what I say.'

'And if you love me as much as you say you do,

you'll let us have something—whatever we can—at least for a while.'

'No, damn it, that's cruel!' She finally found the energy to pull away from him; now she turned on him, trembling, perilously close to the limits of her control. 'Don't you care what you're doing to me? Don't you care that I'm already torn apart? Damn you, O'Neil, I was happy enough until you dropped into my life! I was managing reasonably well; I could accept what was going to happen, and now everything's ruined. I can't bear to try to live with you and I'm too frightened of the surgery even to think about having it done. I don't have any choices left—none at all. You've taken them all away, and I don't know what I'm going to do,' she finished, tears starting.

The next moment she was sobbing, standing defenceless in the centre of that huge room, her hands covering her face as she began to cry out all the pain and anguish and grief. 'Oh, I'm so frightened!' she cried miserably, and kept sobbing, even when O'Neil picked her up and carried her back to the couch.

Once she had started, she couldn't stop. She kept on, choking on her tears while he cradled her in his arms, rocking her back and forth like a child, all the while murmuring soft, indistinguishable words. He loved her, she knew. If nothing else proved it, this did, which only made matters worse. He loved her this much and she loved him this much, and there was absolutely no future for all this love between them. It was worse than death, worse than dying—a hundred times worse—and she couldn't stop crying for all that was lost. She cried for what seemed like—and possibly was—a matter of hours, until she finally slipped unknowingly into the sleep of exhaustion.

When she awoke, she was still in O'Neil's arms, and in the cold light of dawn she could see his face, gaunt and grey with fatigue. He wasn't asleep, and she doubted that he had slept at all. He looked as though he had been through his own hell while, alone in the darkness, he had held her sleeping form. What am I doing to him? she asked herself, thinking of his lonely vigil, then told herself that a vigil of one night was better than a year of watching . . .

Now, in the instant when he realised that she was awake, his eyes grew watchful, cautious and clouded with pain. 'Mari?' he asked, managing only her name.

'I haven't changed my mind,' she told him, her voice a ragged croak. 'I still feel the same way.'

'Yes, I was afraid so,' he acknowledged, and, if her voice had sounded wasted, his sounded dead. 'And nothing I can say will change your mind?'

'Nothing.'

'Then I don't have a choice. I can't do to you what I did last night, can't put you through that again. So——' he stopped, drawing a long and uneven breath '—tell me what you want me to do.'

'Let me go back to Vermont, and don't ever come back to see me. Let it end, O'Neil. Right here. Right now.'

He started to speak—to offer one last argument, she knew—then stopped himself, his jaw clenched with the effort of keeping silent. 'All right,' he managed at last. 'Shall I take you to the airport?'

'No, please don't.'

'All right,' he said again. She could feel the sudden tension in him when she pulled away from him to stand, but at least he didn't try to stop her. 'I'll arrange for the plane, and a car.'

Mari nodded, turning away, trying to find some

distance, some sense of aloneness to see her through these last few meaningless minutes. She didn't succeed, of course, but she found a little safety in leaving him to climb the stairs to his bedroom. There she packed her few belongings, removing every trace of her brief occupancy. By the time she was done, she had managed a little emptiness, and that was enough.

When O'Neil told her the car had arrived, she didn't permit herself to hesitate or waver. She simply picked up her bag, ready to leave, and reached for her bag.

He stopped her then, taking the bag for her and holding it as he looked sombrely down at her. 'Mari, at least tell your family what's happening. Don't leave yourself totally alone with this.'

'No, O'Neil, I can't,' she told him, her voice as empty as she felt. 'I've got to do this my way.' Then she took her bag from him and turned towards the door—never looking back—not even once.

At the airport in Burlington, as soon as Mari entered the terminal building, she heard Lily's voice . . . and froze.

'Mari, I'm over here. Darling, what happened?'

'I——How did you know I'd be here?'

'O'Neil called me. He——'

'*No!*' He couldn't have—could he? *Could* he have so completely gone against her wishes as to tell Lily what was wrong with her? 'What did he say to you? What did he *tell* you?'

'Only that you were coming home,' Lily explained, looking even more puzzled than before, 'and that you'd need someone with you. I don't understand any of this! He sounded terrible, Mari, and you look even worse. What's happened between you?'

Well, at least he hadn't told, but he still shouldn't have called Lily, Mari thought, the emptiness returning. He had broken the rules by calling Lily; he had let what had been happening between them continue, if only for a few hours more. Damn him, she thought dully, keeping silent, ignoring Lily's concerned glances while they made their way out to the car. She should hate him for breaking the rules, but she was far beyond anger, beyond any emotion at all—until she saw Founder waiting in the car.

'O'Neil told me to bring him,' Lily explained as the dog recognised Mari and began to jump against the window closest to her. 'He said you'd need Founder.'

That didn't just hurt, that tore through her, the pain so great that it took her breath away. She bent her head so that Lily wouldn't see her tears, and once in the car she held the dog's squirming body close when he leapt into her lap to lick her face.

'Mari?' Lily waited until they had left behind what passed for congestion in Burlington, waited until they had turned on to the first of the country roads leading home. 'Won't you tell me what's wrong? O'Neil wouldn't say a thing.'

Thank heaven for that. 'We broke up, that's all.'

'That's all?' Lily repeated ironically. 'Don't tell me that's all! Something terrible must have happened, but whatever it was, it *shouldn't* have happened! You wouldn't both be so miserable if you didn't still matter so much to each other.'

'And you're the one who told me not to go to New York with him,' Mari mused, entirely detached from the situation, so tired and empty that she felt like an outsider, someone watching the action from a distance. 'You were right.'

'No, I was wrong,' snapped Lily. 'The man *cares*

about you! If you could have heard him——'

'Oh, I've heard him, all right. I've heard everything O'Neil has to say, but it just won't work. We've got——' Mari paused briefly, amused by the bizarre truth of what she was about to say. 'We've got a basic difference of opinion, and it won't go away.'

'But, Mari, you're so unhappy!'

'At the moment, but it won't last. I'll be back to normal within a few days.'

'Back to that sterile, lonely life of yours, you mean.'

'That's right,' Mari agreed, but with such a cold edge to her voice that Lily was warned off, and they completed the trip in silence.

'I put a few things in the fridge for you,' Lily explained awkwardly when they pulled into Mari's drive. 'They should tide you over until tomorrow morning. I'll stop by then, to see what you want from town. Mari,' she added doubtfully, 'are you going to be all right?'

'Of course.' She watched Founder jump out of the car, delighted to be home again, then followed more slowly. 'I'll be fine.'

'And I will be,' she assured him, moving around her little house when Lily had driven off. The place was stale and airless, and she went around, opening windows. 'The trouble right now is that I'm too tired. I feel as if I could sleep for a week, but I'll be back to normal soon enough. You'll see, good dog.'

It didn't happen that way. Two weeks passed; a month passed, and Mari was as thoroughly miserable as she had been at the start. Each day she went through the motions of living her usual life, and the simple act of being busy insulated her from the sharp pain that caught her unawares whenever she had nothing to do. If she could have filled all twenty-four hours of each day, she might have managed, but there were too many empty hours. There were evenings and nights and the odd moments during the day when she paused in her work and the pain overtook her, still fresh and a hundred times more alive than she was.

'I can't stand it,' she finally admitted to Founder. 'There's got to be some way out, at least some way to *try*!'

But what? She couldn't go back to O'Neil, and she couldn't consider the surgery—not when any thought of it was accompanied by a vision of O'Neil standing powerless by her bed, watching her blank face just as he had once stood by Jill's bed and watched hers.

'So what do I do?' she repeatedly asked Founder—and herself—for the next few days. 'What *can* I do?' And the answer, when it finally came, was so breathtakingly simple that the only wonder was why she hadn't thought of it long before.

It was early October now, autumn in Vermont, one of those glorious days everyone thinks of when they think of Vermont. The maple trees were crimson and gold, the sky a deep and bold blue, the air fresh and lively, almost crackling with the excitement of all the world's beauty. And for the first time since she had heard Dr Horner's words, Mari found herself beginning to feel at least a little alive, found her spirits beginning to lift.

In fact, she found herself feeling positively giddy with the relief of having thought of an answer, at finally being able to act—to *do* something. 'This is a marvellous day,' she told Founder when she had promised him a run and got her bike out of the shed. 'This is just as rare a day as a day in June—as *that* day in June was. And—just maybe—I've found a way to have more days like that,' she finished, and her early afternoon ride through the riot of colour only served to reinforce her feeling of wild optimism.

'Lily, can I use your telephone?' she demanded, bursting into her sister's kitchen, Founder bouncing behind. 'It's a toll call, and it may take forever, but I promise I'll pay you back.'

'You're calling O'Neil! I *knew* you'd come to your senses!'

'No, not O'Neil, but it's nearly as good,' Mari explained obliquely, hugging her secret to herself, realising that it wouldn't do to let Lily hear her end of the call she was about to make. She was going to do this thing alone; only when it was done and she had either succeeded or failed would anyone know. 'Can I use the phone in your bedroom?'

'Of course,' Lily agreed, biting back the questions she longed to ask. For a month she had been watching Mari's misery and aching inside for her sister, wishing there were something she could say or do, but shut off each time she tried to raise the subject. Now, to see Mari suddenly happy—alive—again. 'Darling, when you're finally yourself again, you can do anything you please!'

Alone in Lily and Nate's bedroom, seated on the edge of their four-poster bed, Mari suffered a momentary attack of nerves. What was she doing? she asked herself wildly, and then—before she could think of any more questions to ask herself—she picked up the receiver and dialled.

It took longer than she had expected. There was the need to explain to various people who she was and why she was calling, long minutes on hold as she was passed up the line. Then at last she heard Dr Horner's clipped voice. 'Yes, Mari, I'd expected to hear from you sooner. What can I do for you?'

'The surgery,' she blurted out, wasting no time on preliminaries. 'Whenever you like—if you're still willing to do it, that is.'

'I am,' he answered evenly, 'just so long as you still understand all the risks.'

'Yes, I do.' Did she ever! 'When can you do it?'

'Well, not for a few days, I'm afraid. Perhaps the middle of next week. Can I get back to you when I have a definite date?'

'Not exactly,' Mari objected quickly, imagining just what Lily would make of a call telling her when her sister was scheduled for surgery in New York. 'I'm really pretty out of touch at the moment, but I'll be in New York in the next day or so. When I know where I'm staying, I'll call and leave the number for you.'

'Won't you be staying with Mr O'Neil?'

'No! Absolutely not, and that's the one thing I've got to ask you to promise—that you won't get in touch with him, won't even think of telling him about this. You *must* promise!'

'If you say so,' he agreed without expression.

He probably didn't care about the personal lives of his patients, Mari reflected when she had replaced the receiver. The Dr Horners of this world probably didn't even think about the personal lives of their patients. They weren't interested in people, just in new techniques, new procedures, their professional reputations. They neither knew nor cared that they sometimes presented their patients with terrible —impossible!—choices. And she had made hers.

'Bad news?' asked Lily, studying Mari's face when she came back into the kitchen. 'You look sort of grim.'

'No, not really,' Mari evaded. 'It's just that deciding

to do something doesn't make it easy.'

Which was some kind of understatement, she told herself as she cycled slowly home, Founder running along beside her. She had made her decision and she was going to stick to it, but it had brought a new terror with it. Back at the house, she sat down on the stepping-stone at the door, Founder leaning against her knee as she stared out across the meadow to the line of crimson maples at the far end.

'What am I doing?' she asked Founder, absently scratching his neck, but she already knew the answer. She was giving up the known and familiar present, even if it was a known and familiar misery. In exchange, she was going to risk everything on an unknown and frightening future, and she was going to do it alone.

This way, there was no chance that O'Neil would ever stand by her bed as he had once stood by Jill's. This way, if it worked, she could go to him with forever to offer. And if it didn't work—well . . . at least he would never know; he would be spared the reliving of that particular agony. This way was the right way, and it could only work if she did it alone.

A noble stoic, he'd called her once, and he'd been right about that. Here she was, playing the noble stoic again. It would be so much easier to face the surgery if she had someone there with her to hold her hand and to care—if she had *O'Neil* there with her, but she wasn't about to do that to him. She *had* to do this thing alone, but the thought of it frightened her and made her feel sadness in a way she had never experienced those two emotions before.

Damn him! That was what he had done to her, she thought, crossing her arms on her knees and leaning her forehead on them. Damn the man for teaching her how much easier things were when you didn't have to face them alone. Damn him for teaching her how good it could be when someone cared. Damn him, she told herself again—not in anger, but in pain, missing him more than at any time in the last month.

Beside her, Founder stirred, then whimpered. Mari raised her head in time to see him get to his feet, staring uncertainly up at the sky as he began to pace. No! she tried to tell herself, it's not true—it *can't* be! It's wishful thinking, because you're feeling particularly alone and unhappy. *Founder's* wishful thinking? another, believing, part of her mind sceptically asked. 'It *can't* be true,' the rest of her said aloud in reply. 'Things like this just don't happen!'

But Founder seemed to think that they did. He was even more restless now, still whimpering, still looking up at the sky while his body turned in tight circles, first one way, then the other.

He was wrong. In her heart, Mari knew he was wrong, but that didn't stop her from standing up, her head cocked to one side as she listened. She wasn't sure of the sound; if she was hearing something, it was probably only a truck toiling up a steep hill on the other side of the valley. Still, the suggestion of sound was enough. She was off and running, around the house and into the brilliant yellow of the second growth on the ridge, up the familiar path and out into the still green field at the top.

The field was empty, and beyond stood O'Neil's empty house. It had been that way for nearly a month, since she had heard in the village that Savin and Rule had gone back to New York. 'I hear that the place is going to be up for sale soon,' Betty Varney had told her, fixing her with a dark and curious stare, waiting for a response. But Mari had said nothing. How could she? She had been too busy trying to ignore the cold chill around her heart, trying to tell herself that she was glad O'Neil was really observing the rules.

Now, on this brilliant October afternoon, she wasn't thinking about the rules. She could only wait in an empty field, with the empty house behind her, watching the deep blue sky—equally empty, except for the steadily growing black dot and the faint but unmistakable beat of an engine. She didn't move when the dot became a real object, didn't move when she could eventually distinguish the lazily turning rotor blade. Even when the helicopter finally set down in the field, less than a hundred feet from where she and Founder stood, she didn't move.

She waited while the engine died in a high-pitched whine, waited while the door opened and O'Neil's long form unfolded itself and stepped on to the grass. Then, as he started towards her, she started towards him, the two of them moving slowly, almost cautiously, just at first. Then, as they began to close the distance between them, they moved faster and faster still, almost running by the final moment when he swept her into his arms.

'I couldn't stay away. I'm sorry, my love.'

'No, don't be sorry,' she told him, her face pressed against his shirt, all her defences, her resolve to be strong, stripped away. 'I wasn't doing very well without you.'

'Neither was I. This hasn't been right, love. I couldn't stand any more, and I don't know why, but today—well, today was the end. I just knew I had to come.'

'Did you?' she asked, laughing and crying together, gripping him tightly, hanging on—quite literally—for her life. 'O'Neil, today was the end for me too. I called Dr Horner today.'

'Did you?' it was his turn to ask unevenly, his lips against her forehead. 'Then I chose the right day to come, didn't I?'

'Yes,' she admitted, letting go of everything she had been trying to do. 'And I'm so glad you're here. I didn't want to do it alone.'

'I know, love, and the best of it is you don't have to,' O'Neil told her, lifting her tear-streaked face to his. 'We're together now, love, no matter what happens.'

EPILOGUE

'MARI! If you don't get a move on, you'll be late for your own wedding!' That was her father's deep bass on the other side of the door, easily carrying over the higher, softer voices of her mother and Violet and Lily and Rose. 'You've only got an hour!'

'That's plenty of time, Dad. Don't worry,' Mari called back, not moving, sitting on the edge of her bed in the room she had shared with Lily for sixteen years, until eventually, when Lily had gone off to college, it had become Mari's own.

There really was no need to hurry, she reflected, smiling at her father's impatience. She was ready, except for her dress, now carefully spread across Lily's old bed on the other side of the room.

That dress! she thought, her breath catching. That glorious, beautiful dress! The wedding dress had been one of O'Neil's many acts of faith. She had learned later that while she had still been in the coma during the first few days after the surgery, O'Neil had called all her sewing ladies and given them specific instructions. They were to choose Mari's favourite dress design and to make it up in the pale cream silk organza he was sending up to them. Then they were to use all the skills Mari had taught them to embroider the skirt and the sleeves with whatever designs they thought she would like best.

'He said we could decide,' Lillian Downey had explained later, 'but he did want us to include your dog and a hot-air balloon, so we went over to your

place and hunted around until we found some
sketches of Founder, and that embroidery picture
with the hot-air balloon in it. I hope you don't mind,'
Lillian had apologised, 'but we needed your drawings.
We didn't trust ourselves to get it right, the way you
would. Besides, Mr O'Neil was paying us all such a
shocking amount of money to do the work that we
thought we'd better get it exactly right.'

And they had, Mari thought, her breath catching
again. The skirt was alive with the most delicate of
embroidered designs—Founder and hot-air balloons,
her little cottage and O'Neil's big house, the covered
bridge in the valley, her bike, maple trees, the village
church—where, in something under an hour, she and
O'Neil would be married. There were mountains and
rainbows and flowers—all the designs she had worked
out over five lonely years. It was positively
baroque—more elaborate than anything Mari herself
could have envisaged or would have tried to do—but it
worked. It worked so incredibly well that now Mari
felt properly humbled, to think what a wonderful eye
for design her sewing ladies had had all along.

And O'Neil had made it happen, just as he had
made so many other things happen, done so much to
gather up all the scattered threads of her life. It was
O'Neil, in the five days between his return and her
surgery, who had convinced her that she must tell her
family what was about to happen to her.

'Don't leave them out, love,' he had cautioned.
'They'll want to be with you; they'll want to care, and
it's a little late in the game to be worrying about still
being the baby of the family. You're too old for the
part, and you'll be a respectable married lady before
long. Surely you can trust them and yourself enough
to let them be with you right now. Love, stop being

the noble stoic!'

So she had abandoned the pose and admitted her problem, and felt herself surrounded—but, to her surprise, never smothered—by her family's love and concern. She supposed it was a lot like loving O'Neil—or hot-air ballooning! Once she had stopped trying to fight against what she was afraid of, it turned out to be gloriously right. Then, before the surgery, the decision to let herself be loved was still something new in her life, but she quickly discovered that letting it happen felt incredibly good.

With her family's support and O'Neil's steadying presence beside her right up to the moment they had wheeled her into the operating-room, she had been able to face the surgery without the panicky fear she had expected to feel. She hadn't been happy about it, of course, and she had still been terribly worried about O'Neil, about how he would manage if things went wrong . . .

But things hadn't gone wrong, although she hadn't known it for nearly a week. She hadn't known that she lay in a coma; still couldn't remember—except for a vague and cloudy recollection of the sound of O'Neil's voice—the days when she had been fighting her way to the surface of consciousness. What she *could* remember—what she would never forget—was the day when she finally made it back.

She had opened her eyes, blinked against the sudden assault of the light, and seen O'Neil's gaunt, haggard face and his off-centre grin. 'You see? I told you it would be all right,' he had said hoarsely, his hand gripping hers very hard, and then—although she wouldn't have believed such a thing possible—his grin had increased. 'Guess what, my love,' he had continued, the quick flame of triumph and laughter bright in his eyes, made brighter still, perhaps, by the tears she thought she saw there. 'The day isn't far off when you're going to have to stand up in front of several hundred people and say, "I, Marigold, take thee Angus"—which will serve you right for having such bad things to say about your name and mine!'

'I, Marigold, take thee, Angus,' she repeated now, caught unawares by such a wealth of emotion that it took a moment for the sound of her mother's voice to penetrate her absorption.

'Mari? Darling, I hate to disturb you, but your father's right. You really should be getting ready.'

'Right.' She got up from the bed and opened the door, instantly surrounded by her mother and Violet and Lily and Rose—her three sisters all looking like girls again in the red velvet gowns which had been O'Neil's choice as the only possible colour for the bride's attendants at a Christmas wedding.

As they helped her to dress, Mari felt like the one point of calm in a sea of high excitement. Her happiness went beyond and was deeper than laughter or tears. She had O'Neil and forever—a forever that Dr Horner had assured them could certainly include children. Now, remembering that particular moment, she was so moved that there was no room for the giddiness infecting her mother and sisters.

She was still calm when they arrived at the church in the village, and while she stood, her arm through her father's, at the back of the church. She heard the old foot-pump organ wheeze a surprisingly deft transition from the prelude to the wedding march, watched Violet and Lily and Rose instantly align themselves and start down the aisle.

Then, still filled with that deep, happy calm, she moved forward. Her hand resting lightly on her father's arm, she was briefly conscious of the slight hesitation of her left leg—the only sign remaining of the ordeal of her surgery, and one Dr Horner had assured them would pass in time.

Ahead, all turned towards her, were so many known and loved faces—her sewing ladies, her aunts and uncles, her parents' friends, her own friends and neighbours, O'Neil's friends and the people he worked with, even Dr Horner, she realised with a start. His tall form stood out, and from the expression on his face one might have thought he considered himself personally responsible for the event about to take place.

Which, in a way, he probably was—and so much for thinking that doctors like Saul Horner didn't care about their patients' personal lives, Mari mused in the moment before her eyes sought and found O'Neil in front of the altar, Jack beside him in his role as best man.

O'Neil too had turned to watch her progress, looking incredibly handsome in his cutaway coat and striped trousers—almost like a stranger, she decided. She had never thought of O'Neil as handsome; he had, from the very beginning, simply been O'Neil—an intensely alive and unbelievably caring man who had brought such warmth and joy to her life. And how could she have guessed on that first morning, when he had literally dropped into her life, that their meeting would lead to this moment of joining themselves together? That thought was another to take her breath away, but her calm still held as O'Neil's clear blue gaze followed her to his side.

'Dearly beloved, we are gathered together . . .' The service had begun; the rest of her life and O'Neil's—

their life together—was beginning now. Mari stood at his side, absorbing the words of the wedding service, each word drawn into her calm and strengthening it.

It wasn't until they began to exchange their vows that her composure deserted her. Then, at Father Fisher's direction, O'Neil turned to her and took her right hand in his, saying, 'I, Angus take thee, Marigold . . .'

Her eyes brimming with a bizarre combination of tears and laughter, Mari looked up to meet O'Neil's gaze. You were right, she told him silently. I'm going to have to say it, but *you* had to say it first—which serves *you* right for teasing me about my name and yours!

He knew; he understood what she had told him. She knew by the way his own eyes suddenly filled with the same combination of tears and laughter. They were two of a kind—now and forever—she realised with a new and even deeper sense of wonder and calm.

Now and forever, O'Neil, she told him silently, now and forever. But saying it silently wasn't enough, she discovered, so when her turn came she added the words to her vow.

'I, Marigold, take thee, Angus—now and forever—to be my husband . . .'

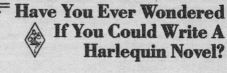

Have You Ever Wondered If You Could Write A Harlequin Novel?

Here's great news—Harlequin is offering a series of cassette tapes to help you do just that. Written by Harlequin editors, these tapes give practical advice on how to make your characters—and your story— come alive. There's a tape for each contemporary romance series Harlequin publishes.

Mail order only

All sales final

HARLEQUIN
American Romance®

THE LOVES OF A CENTURY...

Join American Romance in a nostalgic look back at the Twentieth Century—at the lives and loves of American men and women from the turn-of-the-century to the dawn of the year 2000.

Journey through the decades from the dance halls of the 1900s to the discos of the seventies ... from Glenn Miller to the Beatles ... from Valentino to Newman ... from corset to miniskirt ... from beau to Significant Other.

Relive the moments ... recapture the memories.

Look now for the CENTURY OF AMERICAN ROMANCE series in Harlequin American Romance. In one of the four American Romance titles appearing each month, for the next twelve months, we'll take you back to a decade of the Twentieth Century, where you'll relive the years and rekindle the romance of days gone by.

Don't miss a day of the CENTURY OF AMERICAN ROMANCE.

A CENTURY OF
AMERICAN ROMANCE
1900's

The women...the men...the passions...
the memories....

CAR-1